MW01539232

CARMODY

Tougher than leather, sharper than steel, Carmody was the most dangerous man in the West. This volume contains two action-packed Carmody Westerns by Peter McCurtin—at a fraction of the cost!

TOUGH BULLET

I told him to stay back when he started at me. When he didn't listen, I pulled the .38 and hit him between the eyes with the thick, shortened barrel. It would have been easier to shoot him than to hit him. I hit him again on both sides of the skull, and that stopped him some but not all the way. I belted him across the thick band of muscle where the neck joined the head.

That stopped him, but didn't knock him down. Hands stretched out, clawing, he stood there solid on his feet, the eyes dull but not rolling, and I had to hit him again—once, twice—in the same place before he was ready to fall. There was blood on the face and head and neck and some of it dripped on me when I raised the gun again but didn't use it. He fell back against a heavy chair and broke it before I had to.

THE KILLERS

"You can't win," Fallon said as I backed out of the room.

Going back to jail, I had to admit that Fallon might be right. Maybe Fallon didn't understand my reasons for taking a stand, and maybe I didn't understand all of it myself. But there I was in the middle of something that wasn't rightly my business.

Talking to myself isn't one of my habits; now I said: "Carmody, however did you manage to live so long?"

DOUBLE-BARREL WESTERN

TOUGH BULLET
and
THE KILLERS

— PETER McCURTIN —

LEISURE BOOKS   NEW YORK CITY

A LEISURE BOOK®

September 1989

Published by

Dorchester Publishing Co., Inc.
276 Fifth Avenue
New York, NY 10001

TOUGH BULLET Copyright MCMLXX by Belmont Productions
THE KILLERS Copyright MCMLXXII by Belmont Productions, Inc.

All rights reserved. No part of this book may be reproduced or transmitted in any form or by any electronic or mechanical means, including photo-copying, recording, or by any information storage and retrieval system, without the written permission of the Publisher, except where permitted by law.

The name ''Leisure Books'' and the stylized ''LB'' with design are trademarks of Dorchester Publishing Co., Inc.

Printed in the United States of America.

TOUGH BULLET

Chapter One

I robbed a gambling hall operated by the three Flynn Brothers—Frank, John, Bill—in Hot Springs, Arkansas, and went down to New Orleans to have myself a time. I didn't get as much as I expected—must have been a slow night—but I got eleven thousand, give or take some, and New Orleans was the closest hell town I could think of.

Besides, New Orleans was my kind of town. Even the way things are, you don't find many big towns where the gangs run hog-wild, where the last two Chiefs of Police, Mealey and Hennessy in this case, get themselves sent to Boot Hill; the first by other ambitious lawdogs who wanted his job and couldn't get him to retire sensiblelike; the second by a bunch of Black Hand Italians who didn't like the way Hennessy worked, which must have been pretty good or pretty bad, depending on how you looked at it. From the Black Hand point of view, then a new point of view in the Crescent City, it must have been pretty bad, because one dark night at the corner of Girod and Rampart these Black Handers lay back in the bushes and blew the chief in half with a blast from a double-barrel cut down to eighteen inches, with the stock sawed through behind the trigger, and hinged.

When I heard about it, I decided that sawing the stock and putting hinges on it so it could be carried on a hook under a dust-coat was a new one on me. In New Orleans they called that kind of weapon a Black Hand persuader. I had been using sawed-offs for years, but hinging the stock was a new twist. I decided I would have to try it sometime.

It was my kind of town all right. Chief Henessy lived long enough to say who shot him and a dying declaration is supposed to be iron-clad evidence in any regular court of law, but not in good old New Orleans. The judge was getting set to turn these Black Handers loose to do some more dirty work when a mob of righteous citizens marched on the Parish Prison and strung up and shot down the dirty foreigners. After that things went back to normal.

I wanted things to be normal. I wanted to rest up for a while, not just hole up the way you can in Galveston and Houston. I didn't want to hole up and get charged extra for everything and still have to wonder if the graft I paid the local law was enough to keep them from pulling a double-cross. What I wanted was to walk around free and easy and have myself a time with some of that eleven thousand.

New Orleans was the town for that. They said it was the wildest, most wide-open big town in the South. It was so wild that newsboys didn't try any more to sell papers with hollers of murder, rape or robbery. And that made sense to me, because how could you sell papers with yellow-rag stories of murder and robbery when everybody was murdering and robbing everybody else.

That's just what New Orleans was like when I went down there looking for fun. At the time I'm talking about the only way to tell the city police apart from the street gangs was—the police wore uniforms. Ask a member of the Metropolitan Police how to get from the corner of South Claiborne and Canal to any address on Louisiana Avenue, and you might get told. Or you might get told to go to hell, or you might get robbed, depending on whether the bluebelly was just feeling mean or dead drunk.

Any town with lawdogs like that is a good place for a man on the run. You could get away with anything in New Orleans. The rest of the country might have wanted posters out on you from one end to the other; in New Orleans you were all right as long as you paid your way.

Lord Almighty, I was ready to do that. All I wanted was a good time—you know, the drinking without fret, the women as clean as money could guarantee, the cards honest or fairly honest—and I was ready to pay for it. I was ready to pay the city detective, a big ugly bull in a hard hat, who called on me a couple of hours after I checked into the Hotel Lafitte on Mount

Royal Street. I guess the room clerks in all the hotels were pretty cozy with the law.

I showed the detective a ten dollar bill, and he laughed in my face. "Captin Basso'll be around to see you later," he advised me. "The captain is Chief of Detectives. He's the one who decides if you stay or go. And how much you pay."

The big bastard didn't even ask my name. I didn't give it to him. But I did say I was ready to cooperate with the captain. More than ready. I was looking forward to it.

Crook or not, he was still a detective. You know what he said? He said, "Watch your step, mister."

Captain Basso didn't bother me. When my trigger finger was working right, which was most of the time, I could draw and fire four bullets and put them close together in less than three seconds. I was six-one tall, thirty-seven in years, and one-ninety in weight. Nobody but a liar would call me handsome, not with the knife mark on the left side of my face, and the bullet-nicked ear. I was tough, and I thought I was smart. Well, maybe I wasn't so smart. I got into trouble. It happened this way. There was this whore called Minnie Haha, so help me, who worked in a cathouse on North Franklin . . .

I wasn't suspicious because staying that way can spoil it when you climb into the sweat-sack with a woman. Anyway, I didn't have to be: the minute I hit town I deposited my eleven thousand dollars in one of the new strongboxes in the big steel safe at the Hotel Lafitte on Royal Street. Sure I was drunk—to get drunk was part of the reason I'd come to New Orleans—and right after I got through with the first whore at Queen Gertie's place on North Franklin, the Queen herself knocked on the door of my room, and when I said she could come in she came in fluttering her fat hands, followed by a big black buck in a derby hat and a candy-striped shirt with rosette armbands bunching up the sleeves.

I guess he was about the biggest buck I ever saw. The silk shirt he wore was likely the biggest size they make, but the slabs of muscle across the chest and shoulders stretched it tight, threatening to pop the buttons. At first I thought there was going to be trouble, but you'd think he'd never left the old plantation—he was so goddamned polite.

The black had two bottles, whiskey and champagne, and two glasses. Queen Gertie was all rings and bracelets and powerful perfume. I thought it was kind of raw, her walking in like that, but I guess she was pretty used to that in her line of business.

Gertie was as fussy as the head sandwich-maker at a church social. "No complaints, I hope," she fluttered. "We do try to give satisfaction. Rita is, shall we say, new to the profession, but, well, her heart is in the right place."

I agreed, saying that as far as I knew everything about Rita was in the right place. Madams don't like that kind of talk. Drunk but polite, I said:

"She's a credit to her race. What race is that, by the way?"

"Honduran," Queen Gertie answered. "Rita's from Honduras."

I couldn't think of anything bad about Honduras. If they has asked me to guess where Rita was from I would have said Mexico. But Honduras was all right with me, and I said so. Before I climbed off my Honduran sweetheart, I tucked a five dollar bill behind her ear and sat up in bed. In Gertie's place they had double beds, making it possible for more than one person to sit up at one time. I was stone-drunk, but I still had my dignity. And I still had my guns.

Both were .38 caliber double-action Colt Lightnings, the barrels cut down. One was stuck in the outside pocket of my coat hanging over the back of a chair. That one was for show, meant to be seen like a stick-pin in a necktie, meant to be gone after if trouble started. The other .38 was stuffed under the pillow. I said I wasn't suspicious, and I wasn't—just careful. I sized up the big black. I figured I could get the gun under the pillow before he got the gun in the coat.

But it wasn't like that, not entirely. Before I could ask Gertie what in hell she was doing in my room with two bottles and a too polite black man, she said:

"Won't you have a drink? It's the custom of the house to welcome all new patrons. I was, uh, busy when you came in, and now I'd like to extend the hand of friendship."

Gertie sure was a fancy talker. They didn't call her Queen Gertie for nothing. Maybe she thought she was being too fancy or else the fancy front slipped a bit.

"What'll it be, pardner?" she wanted to know, knowing damn well I was no city boy, maybe wanting to make me feel at home so far East. "What's your pleasure—champagne or whiskey?"

"Both," I said, thinking that only a shit-kicking fool would want a drink like that. "About half-and-half, I guess." It was the kind of thing a drunk, shit-kicking fool would say.

Gertie laughed so hard all her rings and bracelets clinked. "I can see you're a man who likes to try something new. And that's the kind of a man I like. By Christ I do."

Gertie remembered she was a lady. "Darned if I don't," she said.

Close to halfway through the two bottles, with me doing most of the drinking, Gertie got back to the subject of me being the kind of a fella that liked to try something new. But—she shook her fat body at me—was I ready to try something really different. There was this beautiful girl named Minnie Haha, and Gertie swore the name was real—a genuine Indian princess—who had never entertained a man who was able to satisfy her. It was the custom, almost a tradition by now, Gertie said, to offer this wonderful opportunity to any man who looked like he might be able to do it.

"You could be the lucky man, Mr. Carmody," Gertie pushed me.

I was good and drunk. I might have mentioned my name. I was in New Orleans to have myself a time, not to sneak around. But I didn't think I had mentioned the name. It was something to think about later.

Gertie knew she had made a slip, and she covered by laughing a lot. Laughing came easy to Gertie. It sounded like she was laughing. The way her fat face was masked with paint and powder it was hard to tell. When she finished cackling like a randy goose she went back to calling me "Tex" and "cowboy."

"How much will it cost me?" I asked her.

The big black handed me a thin Cuban cheroot and put a match to it. Then he stood back, folded his arms, still as a statue.

More cackling from Gertie. "Not a nickle, cowboy. You can bet me if you like. The sky's the limit, provided you got the money. If you don't want to bet, that's all right, too."

"What's the catch?"

"Mercy me, there's no catch. It's just something special. A specialty of the house. You already paid, didn't you? We got a lot of Texas men here, and they all like to try. Of course if you're not interested . . ."

"Whoa there, Gertie," I stopped her. Most of the hundred dollars spending money I had held out from the elven thousand in the hotel strongbox was left. "Fifty dollars," I said to Gertie. "I bet fifty dollars against your girl."

Gertie said that was fine.

I didn't figure I'd win the contest because old Gertie would never bet on anything but a sure thing. That was jake with me. Let the old bitch take the fifty and laugh herself sick. There was more where that came from, and when that was gone, well, the country was full of banks and gambling halls waiting to be milked.

"Lead me to it," I said.

It must have looked kind of silly, Gertie leading me buff nekkid down the red-carpeted hall, the big black walking behind with the bottles and my clothes. Gertie said there was no need for me to carry the .38 I fetched out from under the pillow. Drunk or not, I saw the sense in that. Even a so-called cold fish like Minnie Haha could get rattled by a client with a gun in his hand.

I gave Gertie the gun.

She led me down the long hall, past the doors behind which the regular clients eased the tension at five dollars a chance. Five or ten at the most was the top price in New Orleans. I guess Gertie missed the good old days right after the war when the Yankee carpetbaggers drove the price up to as much as twenty-five for a girl with no special looks or talent.

Minnie's quarters were on the third floor, two rooms choked with stuffed furniture, the noise from the street deadened by heavy curtains, with an honest-to-God bathroom—very fancy. The lights were electric, in frosted globes, and one wall was taken up by an oil painting of a lot of bare-ass fat women being chased through the woods by a randy-looking little fella with chin whiskers and goat's feet, playing a flute. I thought he would make better time if he got rid of that flute.

Minnie Haha came out of the bathroom when

we came in. She didn't look pleased to see me, and she didn't look sorry. She was dark enough to pass for an Indian if you didn't know what a real Indian looked like. What she looked like was an Indian princess in a dime novel. Graceful and tall, dark-skinned and black-haired, with even features and green eyes. Good looking as hell, not a bit like any real Indian I ever saw.

Minnie was wearing a wispy something that showed more than it hid, which of course was the idea. She climbed on to the big four-poster without saying a word and propped herself up against a stack of silk pillows. The green eyes that looked at me were blank, not cold or mean, just blank.

Gertie spoke as if Minnie needed an interpreter. Or like a schoolmarm taking the fifth grade on a tour of the first Confederate capital at Montgomery. "Minnie doesn't talk much, Mr. . . ."

Gertie paused for my name. I gave it to her.

"But you'll find her a sweet girl, Mr. Carmody," Gertie went on. "Confidentially, Mr. Carmody, Minnie had a terrible experience as a young girl. Which explains everything, if you know what I mean."

"You bet," I said. The booze was getting to me now, and I didn't want to waste another minute. Feeling confident, I started for the bed.

Queen Gertie coughed delicately. "The fifty dollars, Mr. Carmody. You do have it?"

"Sling those pants this way," I told the black. While I was digging out the fifty I felt for the key of the hotel strongbox. It was still there. I put the pants across the back of a bowlegged chair beside the bed and handed the money to Gertie. The fifty was gone then and there, but what the hell!

Gertie tucked it away in the front of her dress. The smile she gave me was motherly. "A drink?" she asked.

I guess I didn't need that last drink. There was most of a quart in my belly. I took it anyway.

"Good luck," Gertie said, and went out, the big houseman behind her. It didn't occur to me to ask Gertie how she planned to judge the contest. The fact is, it wasn't much of a contest. I was ready and raring to go, but that isn't enough sometimes. Not when a man has all that whiskey in his gut. Sure I tried. I tried hard, but it was like trying to swim across the Colorado River in a sack.

"Sorry, princess," I mumbled, trying to look at her through the fog. There was something else in that bottle besides whiskey. I didn't think about that at the time. I didn't think about anything. I wanted to go to sleep. I went to sleep . . .

Chapter Two

When I woke up Minnie Haha was gone. So was the four-poster. Then I realized I wasn't in the same room. There was light coming through the oiled-paper shade on the window. There was a pain like a broken leg in my skull, and shutting my eyes against the light didn't help much. My mouth tasted like dirty socks, and the room stank of perfume and disinfectant and whiskey. The whiskey stink came from me.

What I needed was more whiskey and, by God, there it was! A full bottle and a clean glass standing on a chair beside the bed. The two .38's lay beside the bottle and my duds hung over the back of the chair. When I was able to sit up—it took about two hundred years—I broke the seal on the bottle with my thumbnail and slopped whiskey into the glass.

I had to hold down the first drink. It kept trying to come up, and fighting it to stay down brought the sweat out on my face. After the second drink, I didn't feel any worse than ready to die, and the third made me feel recovered enough to be plain miserable.

Sitting up, I checked the guns. They were all right and the thirty-five dollars in my pants pocket added up right. The key to the strongbox was still there. The look and smell of the room told me I was still in Queen Gertie's. Squinting with pain, I raised the shade, and there was North Franklin Street, deserted and quiet in the hard morning light. About five o'clock, I figured, and except for some loud snoring somewhere, Gertie's place was as quiet as the street.

There was a washstand, a jug and basin on top. I washed my face, left some water in the jug to rinse out my mouth. It took a lot of rinsing to get rid of the bad taste. After that I had another drink and —Gertie was right considerate—fired up one of the good Cuban cheroots lying on the chair.

I dressed and pulled on my boots without making too much noise. The snoring stopped and started again as I went down the hall to the stairs, my boots making no sound on the thick carpet. I wasn't being careful—didn't see any cause to be. All I wanted was to get out of there without having to talk to anybody. To get back to the hotel and sleep till night, or the next morning if I felt like it. I still felt bad enough to shoot myself with my own gun, so it must have been a pretty good night.

There was a big black sleeping in a chair inside the front door. Not the same houseman I'd seen the night before, not as big but big enough, bigger than I was. He was tilted back in the chair so that the pearl handle of a small handgun stuck out of his pants pocket. He didn't stir when I stepped over his feet, opened the door, letting the spring lock click behind me.

Out in the street it was early enough to be cool. A few hours later the July sun would bake the city, soaking the air with water from the lake. It was good to get the cathouse smell out of my lungs, at least for the time being. I walked for a while, then a horsetrolley came clanking by, and I rode that back to the Hotel Lafitte.

There were other hungover gents on the trolley. One of them was a cowman of some kind, leather-faced, eyeballs laced with red, about fifty. He didn't look happy, and it wasn't just the morning after blues. He uncorked the bottle riding in his hip pocket, and when he pegged me for a fellow Texan he shook it at me.

"Want a snort?" he said.

I told him thanks, no.

He had one himself and put the bottle away. The drink made him feel worse, from the looks of things. He spat on the floor between his feet and said to me:

"I tell you, brother, this New Orleans is a mean, low-down place."

The sway of the trolley went against the sway in my head. I was feeling bad, but there were no complaints, not yet anyhow. I thought old Gertie had treated me fair enough by hell town standards—the whiskey, the cigars, the fact that I still had thirty-five dollars in my pocket.

One thing I can't stomach is a whiner. I ig-

nored the son of a bitch. He kept quiet for a
while, but before he swung down from the trolley he fixed me with his bloodshot eyes, and
said:

"This here is a rotten town."

I didn't know how right he was until some
time later. It was about six when I carried my
throbbing head up the front steps of the Lafitte
Hotel. The Lafitte has real white-marble steps.
My skull felt as if it had bounced from top step
to bottom and back up again. The electric chan-
delier in the lobby hadn't been turned off yet,
and it was brighter inside than in the street. The
night clerk was asleep behind the desk, and he
didn't wake up when I went around and got my
key from the ring-board.

The strongbox room was past the desk, between the main staircase and the manager's office. It was long and narrow, and a guard with a
sawed-off shotgun sat in a cage at the end of it.
The guard had nothing to do with the strongboxes except to stand, or sit, guard over them.
The manager rented out the boxes: The customer got a key to his box, and the manager had a
master key to all of them.

The guard was awake, and he watched while I
walked down to No. 37, my box, and unlocked
it. Suddenly my head felt worse. My rifle, gunbelt and .45 were right where I left them, but
the money was gone. I didn't swear, didn't do
anything except look harder inside that box.
Hard or easy looking didn't do any good: The
money was gone, all eleven thousand.

In my line of work you get used to surprises

after the first few. The money comes and goes, and when it goes it's because I spend it or someone gets the drop on me. Usually I spend it, but there have been the other times, and most of the other times I knew who'd done the taking, and went after them with a gun and took it back after I killed them. For me, this was the first time the money just up and walked away with somebody.

The strongboxes were built into the walls, one on top of the other. The door of my box was level with my head. I put my forehead against the steel door, not because I was sick about the money; because my head was sick and the cold steel made it feel better. It didn't make the guard feel better, it made him edgy.

"Something wrong, mister?" he enquired, and brought up the shotgun to show he was worried about me.

The money was stolen, in the first place by me, but I couldn't let it go just like that. I thought of Gertie, the big black, Minnie Haha, too. It seemed reasonable to figure one or two or all had something to do with it. I looked into the close-set eyes of the double-barrel in the guard's hands. "Anybody open my box tonight?" I asked him.

"What box is that?" he said.

"Thirty-seven."

"How should I know?"

There was no point in swearing at a man, even a dumb shotgun guard with a scattergun in his hands, a scattergun level with your belly.

"I know," I told him. "You just watch the

boxes. You don't ask questions." I wasn't as cool as I sounded, but I worked at it. Planning the Hot Springs job took a lot of time—the Flynn Brothers weren't easy to rob—and now the proceeds just up and disappeared. For one reason or other the pickings had been thin the past few months and, damn it to eternal hell, I was looking forward to a good time in New Orleans.

"I been cleaned out," I told the guard. "You notice anybody in here tonight might have done it. My box is thirty-seven. You get what I'm telling you?"

Now the guard was really edgy. He wasn't all that old, but he shook the shotgun like an old man afraid of losing his job. "Stand right there, don't do nothing," he told me in a thin, rattled voice. He rested the shotgun on the bottom bar of the cage, and I could hear a buzzer sounding in the manager's office when he reached under the desk with his left hand. I hadn't moved. "Stay where you are," he warned me.

The night manager came out of the office sleepy and lemon-faced, a young man with a thin, yellow face on top of a fat body. The waxed mustache that separated his nose from his puckered mouth didn't make him look anything but foolish. He needed something to improve his fever-sick face, but it wasn't that mustache.

I guess I didn't look like anything special. He looked past me to the guard in the cage. "What is it, Cappy?" he asked. He forgot about his French mustache and frock coat. "What the hell's going on here?"

The guard didn't explain very well.

"What he means," I said, "is my box is cleaned out. All the money cleaned out. I was asking Cappy here who might have cleaned it out. Not you, I don't expect."

"I beg your pardon," the fool said like a talking peacock. I guess he couldn't think of anything else to say after that. So he said again, "I *beg* your pardon, sir."

"You'll have to do better than that if you took my money," I warned him. "I still have my key, and the box is empty. Maybe you can explain?"

"My dear sir," he blustered, dull spots of red showing in his yellow face. "I am fully bonded by the Holmes Protection Company. As I told you earlier, we cannot be responsible for the loss of valuables by fire, theft or natural disaster. We take certain precautions—the guard—but our liability does not go beyond that."

I wanted to rip off his little mustache like a corn plaster and stuff it down his throat. An explanation was what I wanted, not a sermon. The look on my face took some of the stuffiness out of him.

"You have had the key in your possession at all times?" he asked.

"Maybe," I said. "I guess you got a point."

The manager started to smile, then thought better of it.

I turned to the guard. "How many people been in here tonight?"

"Answer the man," the manager told him.

"Just three. One of them was Mr. Willis. I

know him. He uses the same box here all the time. The other two were together, a man and woman. They were only here a minute or so."

"You aren't getting paid by the word," I snarled at him. "You can tell us what they looked like. If you ever saw them before."

The guard shook his head. "They had a key, and they looked all right to me. They opened one of the boxes—I guess right about where Box 37 is—and then went out. They took something out of the box. I think they did. Maybe they put something in. I didn't pay them much heed."

My head hurt like one big toothache, and it took some doing to keep my temper. "Look," I said. "Were they old, young? Skinny or fat? Did they say anything? To you, I mean."

"I told you," the guard complained. "They just came in and went out. I don't know what they looked like. The woman could have been young. The way she was wrapped up I can't tell you what she was. The man? The man was older. From the way he moved, not from his face. A big heavy man with a wide hat."

A man and a woman. The woman younger than the man. Gertie had called me Carmody when she wasn't supposed to know my name. That didn't have to mean much. The police knew who I was. Captain Basso knew who I was. Maybe he told Gertie. I had gone to sleep in Minnie's four-poster, the strongbox key still in my pocket. Trying to put it all together made my head hurt like a son of a bitch.

The yellow-faced manager stood by, not saying a word. The guard twisted the scattergun in his knobby hands. "The time?" I said to him. "What time was it?"

The guard started off about Mr. Willis.

"The man and woman came in about three," he said quickly. "About three is right. I was eating my lunch. That's how I remember."

The guard looked pleased with himself. The manager told him to get back to his post. He said to me:

"I think I better call the police."

The last thing I wanted was the police. If I was feeling better the idea might have been funny. "No police," I said. "I'll take care of this myself."

The manager got some of his starch back, and the yellow face looked me over, decided I wasn't much. "I'd prefer to call in the police," he said.

"No, you wouldn't," I said. "You just want to look good. Forget the police. You and the hotel are out of this. Unless you happen to be in it personally. If you are, friend, the police won't do you any good."

The yellow face stiffened with indignation, and I expected him to beg my pardon again.

"Go on back and go to sleep," I told him when he didn't say anything right away. "Could be we'll have something to talk about later."

The manager went into his office and slammed the door, and I went upstairs to get a drink. I sat on the edge of the bed with the glass in my hand, cursing New Orleans to eternal damnation. When I got sick of that I corked the bottle, went down to the street, and rode a trolley back to Queen Gertie's place on North Franklin. It was close to eight when I got down from the trolley and walked the extra two blocks to the cathouse.

It was hot, the air full of dust and noise, the street backed up with wagons and buckboards. A teamster who looked like a dressed up gorilla was cursing at an old black woman with a basket of fruit who wouldn't get out of his way. I crossed the street and went up the steps to Gertie's place and pulled the bell. The cathouse was quiet, the shades pulled down against the heat. It took two more pulls on the bell to get the door open.

It was the big black from the night before and there was no expression in his face, no sign that he knew who I was. "We're closed, mister," he said. "Today's Monday and we're closed. Come back tomorrow."

The big bastard tried to close the door. It wasn't easy to keep it open. I had to use my shoulder hard, and when the door started to close anyway I reached into my side pocket for a .38 and showed it to him.

He stepped back from the door, and I walked him backward into the hall. I kicked the door shut with my heel, and put the .38 inside the waistband of my pants where I could get at it in a hurry. The houseman had a polishing rag in one hand, and there was a strong smell of wax. The huge shoulders and the gun I knew he was packing didn't go with polishing the furniture.

He continued to back away from me. "Stay still," I said. When he did that, I asked him if he knew anything about a key to a certain strong-box.

Maybe I didn't ask him right, or maybe he was dumb. I didn't think so. The big man was too mean looking to be dumb. The meanness was all in the eyes: the rest of the smooth black face was just that—smooth and black.

"We're closed Mondays. We're open six days but Mondays is closed." Maybe he thought I was dumb. Maybe he was right, for other reasons. He told me again about Mondays. "Now, sir, you just got to wait till tomorrow. You stay here I just got to summon the police. Miss Gertie ain't going to like this one bit."

"You got a name," I said. "What might it be?"

The big man's dull eyes tried to be as blank as the rest of his shiny face. It must have been an effort because his powerful fingers gathered the polishing-rag into a ball and squeezed it. The voice was kind of high for such a big man. He asked:

"What you want to know for?"

I didn't answer.

"Sam Nails," he said. "Samuel J. Nails."

"I'm Mister Carmody," I said. "You know anything about my key and my money, Mister Nails? You do recall who I am, Mister Nails? Now what about it?"

"This is crazy talk, Mister Carmody," Sam Nails said. "Sure I remember you. You had a good time here. Why, Mister Carmody, it was me carried you from Miss Minnie's room so you could sleep it off. You ain't got no cause to complain, sir. Miss Gertie told me to lay out the whiskey and everything. Wo do right by folks, Mister Carmody."

I asked him where Miss Gertie was, where Miss Minnie was.

"Miss Gertie still asleep," the black said. "Miss Minnie gone off someplace. The rest of the ladies gone, too. In the summer Miss Gertie let them spend Mondays out by the lake. Miss Gertie got a cottage out there. Nice and cool, they tell me."

Samuel J. Nails smiled at me, and he managed to blank out most of the meanness.

I smiled at him. "Tell Miss Gertie I want to see her. Not later, Mister Nails—right now. Yes, I know you're closed Mondays, and I should come back tomorrow, but I won't. Now, Mister Nails."

Nails bunched the polishing-rag so tight I expected to see a handful of dust when he unclenched his big hand. The other hand he unclenched had nothing in it. The rag fell to the floor, and the two big hands turned into sledge hammers. Back where I come from a black man can get killed for a lot less than he called me. I didn't mind 'specially.

I told him to stay back when he started at me. When he didn't listen, I pulled the .38 and hit him between the eyes with the thick, shortened barrel. It would have been easier to shoot him than to hit him. I hit him again on both sides of the skull, and that stopped him some but not all the way. The big hands reached for my throat, and I hit him again on top of the skull. That one didn't stop him either—but it turned his head—

and I belted him across the thick band of muscle where the neck joined the head.

That stopped him but didn't knock him down. Hands stretched out, clawing, he stood there solid on his feet, the eyes dull but not rolling, and I had to hit him again—once, twice—in the same place before he was ready to fall. There was blood on the face and head and neck and some of it dripped on me when I raised the gun again but didn't use it. He fell back against a heavy chair and broke it before I had to.

It was hot and quiet in the hall. Nails might have been dead. I didn't think so. A bluebottle fly buzzed, and I slapped at it with my left hand, and didn't hit it. The bluebottle buzzed away, and I listened for the black's breathing. It was fast and light, peaceful like a man who needs his sleep.

It was the only sound in the house.

Chapter Three

You know how it is when something is wrong. When something—everything—smells and feels wrong. Sometimes you get the bad feeling right away, sometimes it takes a while. Losing the money, knocking down the black, being sick with whiskey and whatever else was in it had sort of blunted me, and I didn't get the feeling till after I checked the rooms on the second floor.

Before I got halfway up to the third floor I smelled death. I didn't smell it: I felt it. There was no smell, but I knew death was up there in the hot, quiet, sweet-smelling gloom. There were no lights burning on the upper floors of the house, and with the shades pulled the air felt thicker and heavier than if the shades were up and the windows were open to let in a breeze.

I remembered where Minnie's rooms were. I drew the .38 and cocked it and turned the doorknob, and when the door opened I kicked it open the rest of the way. I went in not knowing what to find. I found nothing when I turned the switch-knob that started the lights. The big four-poster was made up neat as can be, and the closetful of clothes—dresses and gowns—was just as tidy. The bathroom was empty.

There was only one other door on that floor. The smell of death came through the door. Gertie was in bed—she was on the bed—and she was dead. She wasn't just dead: she was very dead. There was blood every place, on the floor, on the walls, all over the bed. So much blood had been beaten out of Gertie—she didn't look fat any more. I knew it was Gertie by the dress, not by the face: there wasn't much face left. Not much head either—the head was beaten in.

My boots squelched in blood. I stepped back and wiped off the blood on the carpet, most of it. I didn't think it would do much good, but I walked around the pool of blood on the floor and pulled out the drawers of the mahogany dressing table placed between the windows. All kinds of truck spilled out—but no money except some foreign coins electro-plated and made into a bracelet. No eleven thousand dollars.

No eleven thousand dollars in Gertie's clothes closet. Nor under the bed. No eleven thousand any place that I thought to look, and I looked all over.

I went back downstairs and rooted through Gertie's office off the hall, and didn't find anything. Samuel J. Nails was still sleeping easy in a pool of blood, not a move out of him, and I got out of there fast. The polished stand-up clock tick-tocking inside the door said it was eight-forty-five.

I walked back to the hotel. I walked slow, thinking. When I opened the door to my room, Basso, Captain Ned Basso, was waiting for me with a gun in his hand. I wasn't careless. I unlocked the door, and when nothing happened I kicked it open. There was nobody behind the door, nobody facing it that I could see.

There was a closet, a big one, and Basso came out of that while I was pouring a drink, and put the gun on me. It was a short gun, big calibered, what they call a detective special. Basso told me to stand where I was. I didn't think Basso was fast with a gun, maybe not even a good shot even when he had it out. But, Lord, I was tired, not wanting much of anything except sleep and then more sleep. After I slept I wanted to think. Think mostly about my eleven thousand.

"Sure," I said to Basso.

"Hands up high," Basso said. "Move and you're dead."

I looked at him. "Not me, captain. I'm still."

Basso said to drop the guns, to kick them out of the way.

"Good man," Basso said. A thought came to him, or maybe he just said it that way. "You took a long time getting back from Gertie's. I've been waiting nearly an hour."

"I walked," I said. "Was I supposed to hurry?"

There was a creepy feeling moving up my spine, a feeling that I was walking the wrong way in quicksand.

"I wonder you came back at all after what you did to Gertie," Basso said, holding the gun steady on my belly. There was nothing in his face to prove he didn't believe what he was saying. But then a New Orleans city detective would know a lot about lying. "Why'd you have to kill her like that? You must be a real animal, cowboy."

I still had the glass in my hand. Basso told me to put it down real careful. Before I did, I finished what was in it.

"What about Gertie?" I bluffed. "Somebody kill the old gal?"

Basso didn't think much of my bluff. "You sit in that chair, cowboy," he said.

Everybody from Texas gets called cowboy, and I was sick of it. "The name is Carmody," I said.

"I already know that," Basso said. "And I know about the Flynn Brothers, too. They didn't call the law on you, but word gets around. Especially to me. But we'll get back to that later. The manager here fetched me on the telephone. Said you accused him of robbing you. Said you acted real tough about it. I was in his office talking to him when headquarters rang up and said Gertie'd been beaten to death. It appears like Gertie's head nigger woke up right after you did the job and ran out of there. The description he gave fits you like a noose—the scar, the nick in the ear."

I looked at Basso, trying to figure his part in this. Sure he was crooked as they come, but that didn't mean he was mixed up in Gertie's murder. Some crooked lawmen are very good at their job when they get around to it.

"Now, captain," I said. "Why would I want to kill Gertie? It could be I don't even know the lady."

Basso sat down on the edge of the bed, far enough away to make it hard to rush him. Basso was thick-bodied without being fat, and the only place the soft living showed was in his jowly red face. The face was a smooth pink, like an under-cooked ham. It was the face of a man accustomed to hot towels and barbershops. It was the face of a man with a brute temper who had learned to control it over the years.

Basso pushed his thick lips together and blew a breath at me. I guess he thought I was wasting his time. There was no tone in his voice. It came out slow and heavy.

"You killed her because you figured she robbed you. Don't tell me you weren't there all last night. The nigger says you were. The manager and the guard say you got real tough about the money. That would be the Flynn money. It all fits together, Carmody. Maybe Gertie rolled you for the strongbox key, maybe she didn't. The point is—you figured she did. You went back there this morning. First you beat the nigger over the head with the same gun you used to kill Gertie a little later."

Keeping me covered, Basso picked up the .38 with some of the houseman's blood still on it. "This gun," he said, "you should have kept going when you got out of there. Now you aren't going any place but the Parish Prison."

"How do you know the houseman didn't do it?" I asked him.

I don't know why I said it. I just said it. "Or somebody else. A madam like Gertie could have a lot of enemies."

Basso shook his bullet head at me. "You did it, Carmody. It couldn't be anybody else. And you're going to swing for it. Just get up slow and easy, and put your hands behind you."

I tried something else. "What about the money?"

"What about it?"

"I don't have it."

Basso's heavy face didn't change. "That doesn't mean a thing to me. Maybe Gertie didn't take the money. That doesn't say you didn't think she did. That you didn't kill her."

Holding the gun steady, he reached into his back pocket and took out a pair of handcuffs. Handcuffs clinking in a lawman's hand is one sound I don't like. I turned around like I was told, and he went behind me. I didn't move till he snapped the handcuffs around one wrist. I have thick wrists, and he had to squeeze a bit. I grabbed the cuffs and turned on him. The gun went off, and I slammed him across the side of the head. The gun fired again, this time into the floor. I wrestled the gun out of his hand and beat him over the head with it. It seemed to be my day for beating people over the head. Basso grunted, and I let him fall to the floor.

I left the .38 with the blood on it. I took Basso's gun, a Smith & Wesson double-action .45 with a shortened barrel, and the other .38. There was no chance that the two shots from Basso's gun hadn't been heard, and I had to get out of there fast. I ran to the top of the stairs and a man in a derby hat hollered at me from the lobby to stand still. He fired two shots that whanged against the brass stair-rail. A single shot from the .45 scared him back behind a pillar, and I ran back along the upstairs hall looking for the fire stairs.

I knew there would be another man waiting in the alley. If he expected me to be careful coming out he was wrong. I came out that door so fast I nearly fell over my feet. He had his gun out, trying to point it. I fell and rolled as the gun went off. The bullet ricocheted off the brick wall and went back at the detective. It didn't hit him. My bullet hit him low on the arm, and I put another one in the other arm. It would have been easier to kill the son of a bitch, but there was no point in making the New Orleans Metropolitan Police Force any madder than it was now. Before I left the detective with his two broken arms I grabbed the bowler hat off his head and tried it on for size. It wasn't a bad fit—a bit tight—but after I ripped out the sweatband it was better, and I didn't feel like a fool—I didn't have time to feel much of anything—when I ran to the end of the alley and then slowed down to a more or less casual walk about where the alley opened into Mount Royal Street. A hat like that would have gone better with a handlebar mustache. I didn't know how much good it would do me: it was the best I could think of at the time.

Captain Ned Basso's short-barreled Smith & Wesson .45 was in my coat pocket, and I had my hand on it. I stepped lively out of the alley. There was a small commotion in front of the main entrance to the Hotel Lafitte, but I kept going like a man with important business on his mind. Nothing gives a man away as much as trying to walk in one direction while looking in the other, so I didn't do it. I walked away from the hotel along Mount Royal, expecting a detective's bullet in the back with every step, but no bullets came, no hollers either, and when I came to the first saloon I went into it.

I don't know what they called it, and I never did learn the name, but it was a saloon and it was close by, and I went inside. That was a gamble, naturally, like most other things a man does when he's on the dodge, but it's been my experience that usually the law thinks in long-distance terms: it doesn't come looking too close to what it calls the scene of the crime. Of course, if you forget bending the handcuffs over Captain Basso's head and shortening both arms of that detective in the alley, I hadn't committed any kind of crime, by my way of thinking, in New Orleans.

I told the bartender a beer and then a whiskey. The place was crowded pretty good for so

early in the morning, and I had to shove a bit to
make room at the bar. The saloon was on Mount
Royal Street and that should have made it an
inch or two better than the dirty dives in the
Irish Channel, but didn't. It was what they call
ether-beer and the whiskey that went with it
was worse than the beer because you could tell
the water that watered it wasn't even clean
water in the first place.

I decided to stay with the beer. I put my foot
on the rail and told the bartender to sell me a
cigar. The cigar cost more than it would have in
El Paso, where they have to carry everything a
long way. While I was smoking it, and it was
burning down to the end about fifteen minutes
later, a lot of trough-fed fellas who looked like
city detectives, with rippled necks and bulge-
bellies, charged by outside. One of them, a big
Irish bastard with a face redder than his hair,
stopped and came back and looked inside, then
decided he was on the wrong track, and trundled
his lead-loaded ass after the rest of them.

A tall geezer who seemed to know everybody
walked into the saloon. He had a shiny rubber
collar, glazed white and dirty, and a tie with
snail tracks on it, and there was a small disagreement with the bartender about putting his
morning whiskey on the slate. All newspaper re-
porters run off at the mouth; this one did.

The bartender still didn't want to extend his
credit. "I suppose you don't want to know about
Gertie neither," the newspaperman bragged.
"Your friend and mine—Queen Gertie," the reporter said. The cigar in his face was cold and

39

short, but he tried to puff on it. He opened his coat, dug his thumbs inside his vest holes and snapped his galluses. The son of a bitch smiled what he thought was a mysterious smile.

I guess it was the smile got him the whiskey. The penpusher snapped the glass of rotgut against the back of his throat, wiped his cigarette-yellow mustache, and tried to weasel a second drink out of the bartender.

The bartender shook his head. "Come on, chum—what about Gertie? Don't tell us she's dead—we know that."

A man at the bar bought the reporter another drink. The news hack liked having an audience. "A dastardly deed," he announced. "I have just telephoned the terrible details to my newspaper. The good lady was beaten to death—her skull crushed by the savage blows—blood everywhere. The work of an inhuman monster, in my opinion."

I ordered another beer and sipped it. I didn't think there was anything new to be learned from the booze-sucking reporter, but I didn't want to get back on the streets just yet.

The bartender drew a beer and shoved it at the reporter. "That's the limit," he said. "Now get on with the story or get the hell out of here."

"They say some cowboy did it," the reporter said. "That's what my good friends in the Metropolitan Police tell me. Some cowboy named Cassidy or Cafferty. No, it was Carmody. He killed poor old Gertie. Thought she'd taken his bankroll. But they'll catch him, mark my words.

they got the whole force looking for him now. Dear old Gertie will be sorely missed."

"Not by me she won't," the bartender sneered.

The man who bought the reporter his second drink resented that. He called the bartender a no-good son of a bitch. The bartender took an ash club from under the bar and showed it to him. He tapped it on the wood to show how nicely it bounced. Some of the drinkers sided with Gertie's protector, some with the bartender. I figured it was time to get out of there before they started taking the place apart.

The first thought I had was to get the hell out of New Orleans. After what I'd done to Basso and the detective in the alley, and especially after what they said I'd done to Gertie, every bull in New Orleans would be looking to kill me. But I'd been hunted before by city police, and I figured I could get out of town, if that was what I wanted to do. Out of New Orleans was sure as hell where I wanted to be, but I wasn't going to run, not yet anyway. Lawmen all over wanted me for a lot of things, and I'd done most of what they wanted me for, but I wasn't wanted anywhere for beating an old woman to death—nowhere except New Orleans, that is. I'd killed men and robbed banks and other places where they keep money, but there were people who took my word when I gave it. I didn't figure my word would be worth much if I got the name of a woman-killer, and the New Orleans law made it stick.

I walked out of the saloon and climbed aboard

41

a horsetrolley going in the direction of North Franklin Street. How to clear my good name—isn't that a laugh—was something I hadn't figured out yet. I hadn't figured it out even a little bit. All I knew was, the whole thing was tied in with Gertie's place. At least, I thought it was. The law might still be watching the place, and they might not. There was nothing I knew for sure. Sam Nails, the big black houseman had some interest for me. So had Minnie Haha, so-called. So had Captain Ned Basso. It could be any or all of them, or it could be somebody I didn't know, hadn't met, might never meet. I went back to North Franklin because it was the only place I could think to start.

I was getting to know that part of town, and I got off the trolley four blocks from Gertie's place and walked the rest of the way. The only law I spotted was an old beer-fattened uniformed bull swinging his club. The bowler hat must have made me look like a potato-eating citizen; he didn't even look at me. Gertie's place looked quiet, all the shades pulled, no sign of a detective watch inside or out. Just to be sure, I went into a saloon across the street and down a bit, but from where I could sit at a table and drink whiskey and watch the cathouse through the open door.

Chapter Four

I gave it some time. I drank whiskey and watched the locked-up whorehouse and thought about my eleven thousand and wondered how in hell I was mixed up in this. It was a fancy saloon, with waiters. "Terrible, ain't it?" my waiter said when he brought the second drink.

I nodded.

"The man did that should be lynched," the waiter said.

"I say he should be castrated and burned," I offered.

I gave the waiter money, and he went away. Three drinks used up thirty minutes, and I thought I might as well get started. There was still no sign of any law, and in a way that made sense. Old Gertie would be in the City Morgue by now and there wasn't a whole lot more the law could learn by poking around in her room. And, unless I was way off in my reckoning, they'd be looking elsewhere for me. That was

43

how I figured it. I didn't figure it for sure. I knew they might be waiting right inside the front door, waiting to kill me.

I walked down the street from the saloon, then crossed it. I hoped I looked something like a city detective in that hard, curve-brimmed hat. I crossed the street, and nobody shot at me. Up the steps I went and pulled the bell.

The door was heavy oak with a peephole set at eye-level. I set myself so the hard hat was about all somebody inside could see. A quiet clicking sound told me the peephole was open. The voice inside was black and maybe it belonged to Samuel Nails.

"Detective Fitzpatrick," I mumbled, trying to speed up my slow Texas talk.

I guess the hard hat fooled him. It was Sam Nails, not looking overcome with grief, and I lined up the heavy Smith & Wesson with his heart, not wanting to drag it out if I had to kill him. There was a bandage wrapped around the big houseman's head, and I guess his head hurt pretty bad, because it took him a while to see who I was. I got ready for a rush, but he didn't do anything but smile at me, and that was something I didn't expect.

"Back off," I said. "Back off, then stand still. One move you're dead."

When I put a gun on people I don't try to scare them; I show them the gun and tell them the facts. After that they can decide whether to be scared or not. One thing was sure—the big black wasn't scared. But he did what he was told: he backed off. And he smiled.

I knew the law could have set up Nails to answer the door. The law could be waiting at the top of the stairs or in Gertie's office off the hall. But the house was quiet and hot and silent; a stand-up clock ticked, and that was all.

I backed Nails into the waiting room where the customers on a normal business day picked the girls they wanted to have. Nails sat down when I told him to, still showing all his sugarcane teeth in a mad dog grin.

"What can I do for you, sir?" the big bastard asked.

I didn't mind him being brave. I just wasn't in the mood for any smart talk from a foxy black. He smiled at me, and I smiled at him. I don't like to call any man a dirty name unless it gets me what I want to know, if it riles him up enough to say what he's hiding, if it knocks him off balance. I called Mr. Nails a dirty nigger. I said he was a dirty nigger, that I meant to beat the shit and the truth out of him.

Mr. Nails dropped his eyelids over his eyes, and that was all. The smile stayed where it was. Nails didn't have much accent of any kind but now, when he answered me, his deep voice sounded like a blackface funnyman in a minstrel show.

"Beggin' you pardon but thass all Ah is—a pore humble black ugly nigger, massa," Mr. Samuel Nails told me. "Now I jus' ast the gemmen wus dey sumpin' Ah could do to hep?"

I tried again. "That sound more natch'rel, Sambo," I said.

"You white son of a bitch," Mr. Nails said, all

the calm gone out of him, and all the country nigger accent. "You murdering white bastard son of a bitch."

"Don't repeat that in Texas," I said, feeling better. "I don't mind especially, but other folks might."

That was supposed to bother him some more. It did. He got so mad that some of the country accent came back. "You're not in Texas now, Carmody. Maybe it's time you went back there."

That told me something—not much. "You don't want to see me caught and hung, Mr. Nails? The fella that killed your friend and benefactor?"

No more smiles from Mr. Nails. "Gertie was white like you. I don't see I owe that woman a thing. You want to kill her—that's your business. The police don't want me—they want you."

"I think they want you," I said, trying something out. "I think you killed her. Anyway, you could have killed her. Did you kill Gertie, Mr. Nails?"

"No, sir, Mr. Carmody," the black said in a bland voice. "You can beat it out of me, and I'll still say no. Least of all, you can *try* to beat it out of me."

I said I wouldn't try—I'd do it.

"No, sir, Mr. Carmody, you won't," Nails said. He put down his arms. I didn't tell him to put them up again. I wasn't sure he'd do it, even with the gun on him, and I didn't want to press the point just yet.

46

"I still think you did it," I said.

Nails smiled again. "That's just talk, Carmody. Texas talk. A white woman gets herself murdered, so naturally a black man did it. That might work in Texas, but this is New Orleans. It's not much better, just a little, just enough to make a difference. The police know I didn't kill Gertie."

I asked him how they know.

"Because you did it," he said.

"This is getting us no place," I said. "Tell me something, you think Minnie Haha might have something to do with it? Maybe Minnie resented all those bulls Gertie set to riding her. She seems kind of refined for a whore."

Nails' eyelids dropped again; his face stayed the same. I didn't know how to take him. That he wasn't afraid of me didn't have to mean anything except that he was big and tough and smart, and had been hiding it for a long time. Maybe he didn't think he had to hide it from me, because I was worse off than he was.

"What about Minnie?" I asked. "You think maybe she was the one stole my key and took the money?" I had tried throwing a scare into Nails and hadn't done so good. Maybe I'd do better later, if nothing else worked. Now I tried money. I told Nails I was fixing to get the eleven thousand back. I said I didn't care how many people I had to shoot to do it. "You talk straight," I said, "and you can name a price."

"Sorry I can't help you, Carmody," Nails answered, the same wide grin on his black face. "Like the man said, I just work here."

I held the Smith & Wesson steady on his heart. "Get up," I told him.

Nails took his time, but he did it. "You ain't going to beat me twice," he said, arms loose by his sides.

"Sure I am," I said. "And you're going to take it. Come on over here, Mr. Nails, and we'll see if maybe you won't change your mind."

I told him to turn around. There were better ways of making him talk, but there wasn't time. Nails stood with his back turned to me, heavy and solid. I hit him across the kidneys. I hit him as hard as I could with the heavy .45. It should have bent him over with pain. All he did was grunt. The next time I hit him in the same place he didn't even grunt. When I hit him again he cursed. That was better.

"Let me know when you get tired," I said.

Hitting a man in the same spot can numb the pain after a while. Few things hurt worse than having your ear slapped against the side of your head with a gun barrel. That's what I did to Nails. The big bastard had a skull like iron. There was a clunking sound and his ear began to puff up. I reached out again to hit him on the other ear, and quick as a mountain lion his left hand clamped around my wrist, and he tossed me over his hip in a forward wrestling pull. It was like being hit in the side with a tree. The gun was still in my hand when I hit the floor. I don't know why it was; every bone in my body felt like it was jerked loose from the other. Anyway, it didn't do me any good. Nails kicked it out of my hand before I could get set to shoot him. My goddamned wrist felt broken, and a fierce pain ran clear up to the shoulder. Nails came at me with another kick, this time aiming for the crotch.

After a kick like that a man is finished for a while. Nails didn't get to land it. I got out of the way fast, backing off from the big bastard. He came at me again while I was reaching for the .38 in my coat pocket, and there wasn't time to get the gun out. I don't know where Nails learned to handle his fists, but he was good. While I was blocking one punch, he rocked my head twice with his left hand. I kept trying to back away, but he came after me, and finally there was no more room to go any place. The door to Gertie's office was closed, and my back was against it.

I could hear my breath rasping in and out of my chest. Nails' grin stayed big and wide no matter how hard my fists smashed him in the mouth. There was blood on my right fist, and most of it was mine—from the torn knuckles. Grinning, Nails stopped blocking the punches I fired at him. He just took them wherever they landed, grunting when the hurt was bad but laughing all the time. Nails had height and weight on me, and reach, and all that long-buried hate for whites and for himself, too, put a driving force into those thick arms and rocky fists. I tried to knee him between the legs, but he blocked it. I swung my fist sideways, like an axe, and if his neck hadn't been short, the powerful shoulder muscles reaching up to support his bullet head, the blow could have broken his Adam's apple and killed him.

I knew I had to get at the .38 or he'd kill me. My hand went into my pocket and took hold of the gun. I didn't bring it out fast enough, and Nails' huge hand clamped on to forearm, the fingers digging in deep. He hit me high in the chest with the other hand, the hardest blow he could deliver, and the door to Gertie's office broke off the hinges and hit the floor with me on top of it. Nails jumped after me, but his foot caught on the bottom of the wrecked door, and fell to one side of me. The fall didn't bother him at all. But it lost him time. I had the .38 out when he rolled on top of me, using his weight to crush the fight out of me. The big bastard nearly got me again. He caught my wrist just as I pressed the muzzle of the .38 against his heart. There was no feeling in my hand, and in another second the wrist bones would snap. I didn't feel my finger squeezing the trigger. It must have, because there was a dull, muffled sound, like when you use a small dynamite charge to kill fish the easy way in a deep pool, except it was a smaller sound than that—much smaller. A .38 doesn't make much sound compared to a .45. When it's dug into a man's chest it makes hardly any noise at all. Even so, it killed Sam Nails instantly. The huge black body quivered just once, a great shudder like a horse dying, and then I was lying under close to three hundred pounds of dead man.

It took some work to roll Nails over on his back. The hole in the front of his black coat was small, with hardly any blood yet, and when I got him off me he didn't look dead. The grin was still on his face when he died; now it was turning into a dead man's grin. You can tell after you've seen enough of them. I didn't look at Nails right away, because I didn't—I couldn't—get up. It was a while before I was able to get up, and after I was up I had to hold on to the back of a chair.

The top of Gertie's desk was rolled down. I rolled it up and found a half-full bottle of brandy. A glass sticky with stale brandy stood beside it. I bypassed the glass and drank from the bottle. Any kind of brandy isn't my drink—too sweet and smelly—but Gertie's brandy sure as hell felt good once it reached my belly. On top of the saloon slop already down there, it buzzed in my ears before it made me feel better. It had to work hard to make me feel better just then. Here I was with the pie knocked out of me, standing over a dead black man I'd just killed, with my eleven thousand still gone and no more likely to come back than five minutes before, and the whole New Orleans Police Department still looking for me, and I knew as much, which was nothing, as I'd known when I walked into Gertie's bedroom and got my boots bloody.

Lord knows I didn't want to go through the dead man's pockets. I wasn't just battered and still hungover; what I was, was tired in the head. Most of all, what I wanted was to dodge on out of New Orleans and put as much distance as I could between me and Whoreville on the Big Muddy. Another drink got me back on the track, and I dug through the dead man's pockets. Nothing but some keys and a five dollar bill and a clipped-out newspaper ad for a Chicago mail order divinity school turned up. The ad said anybody could get a doctor of divinity degree, complete with scrolled parchment, regardless of race, original religion, or lack of formal book learning. The ad didn't exactly fit with Mr. Nails' old job with Gertie. Or maybe it did.

What I didn't find was my eleven thousand dollars or any part of it, or any sign that the dead man had anything to do with taking it. That made me want another drink, but I let it go, and went upstairs to have another look through Minnie Haha's room. I didn't know how much time I had. Captain Basso and his bulls might be on their way, for all I knew. Gertie might have a partner I didn't know about. They might come one at a time or all together.

Minnie's room was the same, dark and quiet, and it didn't stink of heavy, cheap perfume like the rest of the house. There was perfume in the room; it was light and easy to take. Except for the clothes in the closet, there was no sign that anybody lived or worked there. A real neat room, elegant and nice, not like a whore's room at all. Not like anybody's room, I decided after looking around. Either the room had been cleaned out, by Minnie or someone else, or else I wasn't looking hard enough.

I sat on the edge of the big bed, thinking. There were no photographs, books, or keepsakes of any kind that I could see. Some people have no use for clutter, but I knew that everybody keeps *something*. Like a detective in a dime novel, I pulled out all the drawers from a dresser and looked inside. There was a big brown envelope lying on top of the plywood divider between the drawers. There were three letters inside, all addressed to Miss Frances Verrier, c/o General Delivery, G.P.O., New Orleans.

I wondered how Miss Frances Verrier got to be Minnie Haha. Naturally, the Minnie Haha was Gertie's idea, not a bad one either, if you ran a whorehouse, but that didn't explain a thing. The letters were postmarked St. Phail, La., a place I didn't know, and they were from Minnie's brother George. The letters whined a lot and more or less said the same thing. Life hadn't been going good for Minnie's brother—I still thought of her as Minnie—or so he said. He said it a lot. It took him pages to say it. Most of the land had been grabbed by the sheriff for back taxes and if the big house didn't get repairs soon the roof would fall in.

I didn't know George Verrier, and I didn't like him. The son of a bitch kept asking if, for God's sake, Minnie couldn't raise some money in New Orleans. On toward the end of each letter George said he hoped the city doctors could help Minnie with her "terrible affliction." He had a lot to say about hard times, not much about Minnie's "affliction," and I wondered what in hell it was. I didn't think it was what Gertie said it was, because I knew Brother George would never talk about something like that, in person, or in a letter.

I put the letters back where I found them and

tried to put some of the pieces together, that is, if the pieces had anything to do with me. Minnie wasn't Minnie. She was Frances Verrier, from St. Phail, Louisiana. She was from good family, and she had a "terrible affliction" and a weak-kneed brother named George who kept asking for money to save the old plantation. Brother George didn't mention any plantation, but I thought of it that way. It had to be some kind of rundown plantation, the way he wrote.

My head hurt. Just because the old Verrier place was going to wrack and ruin didn't have to mean that Minnie clipped my eleven thousand to save it. The "terrible affliction" was what interested me. I don't know why, but somehow it didn't sound like consumption or any other sickness I could think of. It wasn't working in a whorehouse either. One thing was plain—Minnie didn't enjoy her work. Sweet Savior! How my head hurt!

I heard the front door click open three floors below. It was that quiet in the house. Right after the click came a scream. I went out of there fast, soft-footed on the thick carpet, down the stairs, the Smith & Wesson in my hand. From the second floor I could see down into the lobby. What I saw was Minnie Haha—Miss Frances Verrier—looking at Sam Nails' body in Gertie's office. Then she heard me, and then she ran for the front door. I could have shot her. There was no point in that. I yelled at her, and she didn't stop. The front door slammed open and stayed open. Two jumps took me down to the first floor, and I went down the front steps even faster.

There was no sign of her in the street.

Chapter Five

Out in the street, I kept going. The waiter who had served in the saloon and another man came out and looked after me. A horsetrolley rattled past as fast as a horsecar can go, and I ran after it and climbed aboard. After about ten blocks I got off it and went into a saloon. The waiter looked like what they call a police buff. Unless I was wrong, he'd be on the telephone to the police right about then.

I nuzzled a beer until I heard the next trolley. The man on the trolley told me I had to change to another car to get to the Irish Channel. There was an old West Texas stage robber named Gordy Hindman who ran a saloon there and might still be alive. Hindman was too old or too old-fashioned to make the switch from stages to trains when robbing the puffers became the new thing to do. Hindman always worked alone, and I guess one man has a hell of a time robbing a train all by his lonesome. Hindman was still wanted for four or five killings, and the last I'd heard of him he was running some kind of saloon in the Channel and going by the name of Corley Harkins. I wasn't any kind of friend, but I knew him—and he owed me a favor. More than ten years before I had saved his life in Hank Tuttle's Perfect Palace Saloon in El Paso when a bunch of drunken bluebellies decided to celebrate the Fourth by kicking him to death. I wouldn't have looked to press the favor if I wasn't in trouble. I wouldn't even have thought of the old thief if I wasn't in trouble. And I knew goddamned well the favor might not mean a thing to him, not with the kind of trouble I was in.

I didn't get to change trolleys right away because the one I was on was held up by the one in front. Detectives in the same kind of hard hats I was wearing were dragging the men passengers off the first trolley and looking them over good. They didn't bother my trolley at all. The law, most of it anyway, and it's something for which I am thankful, is like that. It gets a fact and holds on to it, tight as the grip of a Gila monster, such as, for instance, I was supposed to be on that first horsetrolley, so, naturally, I couldn't be on the trolley behind it, or any other trolley in the City of New Orleans.

I guess Captain Basso might have thought of that, but that crooked bull wasn't there. I had the feeling he'd be coming after me once his head felt better; he wasn't there at the time. They let us go on after a while, and I changed cars at Loyola Street and Jackson Avenue, and rode the Jackson Avenue Street line down to Constance Street, and got off. More or less, the Irish Channel was between Constance Street and the river. Sideways, the Channel ran east from Louisiana Avenue. I knew that much from old stories. There were a lot of wild stories about Micktown, and I knew some of them. What I didn't know was where Corley Harkins, to name him new, had his place, if he had a place, if he was still among the living.

A rat-faced bastard in a dirty shirt, with a toothpick in his mouth, told me he never heard of no Corley Harkins. The jasper with the toothpick was standing on the corner of Jackson and Annunciation, and the toothpick was just front, because he had no teeth to go with it. The son of a bitch had an Irish accent and the temper to go with it, and knowing about things like that from experience and hearsay, and being on the run, I didn't attempt to teach him better manners. I think he wanted me to try. Soaked in water, which would have been a new experience for him, he must have sunk the scales at all of a hundred-forty, and he still wanted to pick a fight.

That's what the Channel was like—that and the two saloons on every block on both sides of the street. I walked around, up one street and down another, thinking maybe I could find Hindman-Harkins place of business. I didn't find it. I walked along St. Thomas Street, along Corduroy Alley, which is supposed to be the toughest part of Irishtown, and that's hard to argue with or to go against, because it's all—or it was—a dirty, stinking hellhole. I passed places called The Pride of Erin, Corny Kelleher's Keltic Kitchen, The Shamrock, Robert Emmet's, Lord Edward Fitzgerald's Beer Parlor & Dance Hall, Vincent Edward McGovern's Olde Irishe Tavern, Malachy MacBrien's Trinity Gardens, and, of course, Mike Murphy's. I didn't think any of them belong to Corley Harkins, but, then, I had no way of knowing.

An old woman with a red nose and a shawl I asked and got told I ought to be ashamed of myself, bothering decent folk, and me a strong, young fella ought to be doing something. I didn't know what something better was in the Channel; maybe it was knocking somebody on the head and taking his poke.

You know what I did, finally? I did what any hayseed does in the big city—I asked a policeman. The bluecoat wasn't more than three quarters drunk, and there were buttons missing off his uniform, top and bottom, but I guess the whiskey was flowing right that day, because the old thick-bodied bull didn't try to hold me up for anything bigger than a cigarette before he accepted one of Gertie's cigars instead and told me I could find Mr. Corley Harkins, Esquire— that's what he said—at the Patrick O'Paso Saloon on Claffey Street.

The bull was at peace with the world, and he told me Patrick O'Paso's served the best drinks in the Channel, hardly a trace of water in the whiskey, and the free lunch didn't stink worse than a soldier's socks.

The bull looked at me, but I guess he didn't

see me any too well. "I have me doubts that
Corley Harkins is Irish a-tall," he said, and that
was pretty powerful praise from a lawdog with a
brogue as thick as mulligan stew.

I found Claffey Street, and I found Patrick
O'Paso's Saloon. The street was more like an
alley, and the saloon wasn't much to look at.
Not much, anyhow, for a man was said to have
taken such heavy money from the stage lines all
over the southwest, over such a lot of years.
Business was good when I went inside, the ta-
bles crowded with spenders and girls in tights
helping them spend. I just about had to fight my
way to a place at the bar, but the barkeep at my
end smiled quick at me when I did find a place;
and he drew me a beer even faster when I said a
beer was what I wanted.

"Like to see Corley," I told him.

He had a wide pink face going white like a
cooked and partly eaten ham—after the feeders
leave the parts they don't like, and the meat
gets dry. A somewhat eaten ham with damp rib-
bons of white hair on top, with unworried wrin-
kles in front under the hair, smart pig eyes and a
pig's mouth.

"So would I," he said, smiling like a city bartender. "Mr. Harkins ain't been in much lately."

I was tired, in trouble. Mostly I was tired of
New Orleans. I knew he was lying. Maybe it was
the detective's iron hat. It was kind of a silly
way to talk. I said: "Listen, sow-face—here or
not, you tell Harkins Carmody wants to see him.
Mention the Fourth of July, 1880—he'll understand."

"This way," pig-face said when he came back. He jerked his pink thumb at a door at the end of the long bar and behind it.

By Christ, there was old Gordy Hindman himself behind a desk that didn't suit an old stage line robber. I don't know how old Gordy was when he retired and put his cache together and headed east to New Orleans. I don't know— maybe fifty-five, maybe older than that. Maybe he was sixty and if that was so, now he was seventy after ten years—and looked eighty. Either he was sick or city life didn't agree with him, which to me was the same thing.

The pig-faced bartender unlocked the door to the office, and after I was in he locked it again. The office behind the saloon was a lot fancier than the saloon itself. Gordy Hindman—Corley Harkins—was fancier than I'd ever known him. Old and fancy. The fancy couldn't hide the old, the tired.

It took him a while to say, "Hello, Carmody. Still a big hit with the ladies, I hear."

The old thief's cackle turned into a fit of coughing that threatened to kill him. He mopped his mouth with a handkerchief that looked like a small tablecloth. He still wanted to enjoy his joke this time he cackled more carefully.

"Not to mention the Chief of Detectives. The son of a bitch!" Hindman added, screwing up his watery eyes. "You should of finished Basso when you had the chance. 'Stead of just breaking his head."

There was a sideboard with bottles on it. I helped myself. On Hindman's desk there was a half-eaten bowl of oatmeal and beside it a glass of milk. The old bastard licked his lips when I threw back the whiskey.

"Word sure gets around," I said. "The whole thing didn't happen more than a few hours back."

"Gertie was kind of a prominent citizen," Hindman said. "People just love a dirty murder. Captain Basso's a prominent citizen, too. Not to mention yourself."

I put more whiskey in the glass. "I didn't kill Gertie," I said.

"Sure, Carmody. It's no skin off my ass. You want me to help you get out of the city, is that it? I guess that can be arranged, for old times sake."

"That isn't what I want," I told him. "What I want is information. Maybe some money. You think old times are worth that much?"

"You think I owe you something?"

"That's up to you."

I figured I'd rob him if he said no. And kill him if I had to.

Maybe he knew what I was thinking. Most likely that's what he would have done in my place. What he said was, "I owe you a favor. One favor. But I'll be the one that decides how big. I ain't scared, you understand. I'm too old and sick to be scared. More tired is what I am. Take a tip from me, Carmody. Get yourself killed before the time comes for oatmeal."

"That won't be for some time," I reminded him. "Now you want to listen or not?"

Having me around made the old thief's stomach act up. He sucked on his milk while I outlined the business with Gertie and the other business with Basso and Sam Nails that came after it.

Just hearing about it seemed to cheer him up. He wheezed at the fun of it. "Lord, but you been busy," he said. "Basso's going to chase you good. Now what was that whore's name again? I guess I heard of that one."

"I told you. Minnie Haha was the name Gertie gave her. The real name is Frances Verrier. With a brother George still lives in a place called St. Phail. You know where that is?"

"That's over in Vernon Parish by the Texas line," Hindman said. "A post office and a few houses. That's all I know about it. You think maybe she went back there?"

I said I didn't know. From the tone of brother George's letters, it didn't look like Minnie was all that strong on making visits to the old homestead. But now that I wanted to have a talk with her, going back home might not seem such a bad idea. Maybe her so-called terrible affliction, whatever in hell it was, would keep her in New Orleans. There was the whole goddamned city to hide in, and I didn't even know my way around.

Hindman looked cagey. "What makes you think I can help you find her?"

"Because I figure you aren't altogether retired. I figure you got some other interests in town besides the saloon. You may be old and tired, Gordy, but you're still a crook."

Hindman liked to hear that. It was like telling

another man he was a credit to the community. "Well, you know how it is, Carmody. A fella has to keep his hand in."

The thing was dragging on too long. "What do you think?" I asked him. "Can you find her without the police tagging along?"

Hindman looked sour, like a seventy-year-old baby. "Don't tell me my business, Carmody. I was fooling the law before your momma dropped you. Let me tell you something else, boy. The big city don't suit you one bit."

"Don't I know it," I agreed.

"Just so you know it, boy," Hindman said, back in cackling good humor. He rooted in the bottom drawer of his desk and came up with a book with a blue cover. He shook it at me. "This here's the New Orleans Blue Book," he said. "New Orleans got it all over New York and Chicago when it comes to Blue Books. This here book's got every quality whore in the city. Measurements, the color of her eyes, the things she'll do for a fella. Didn't know there was a picture book like that, did you?"

He was right. I didn't.

Hindman flipped through the book, muttering as he did it. "This the girl?" he asked, and there was Miss Frances Verrier lying on a leopard-skin rug and wearing nothing but stiff smile and a wisp of gauzy cloth.

Looking at Minnie made Hindman reach for his tablecloth of a handkerchief. He mopped his mouth. "Dark meat," he said. "Real juicy little Creole."

He tore the picture out of the book. "Should

be a help finding her," he said. "When you talk to her, ask her if she'd like to come and work for me personal. Don't you kill this one, Carmody."

I wanted to get on with it. I guess so did Hindman. He quit making the bad jokes and turned sour again. "One favor, Carmody—that's the limit. Give you some money and find the girl if she's in town. After that we're even. Don't come around again, no matter how bad it gets."

"Fine by me," I said. "How much money?

"Two hundred. Two-fifty. You don't break loose on that, friend, you ain't going to break loose at all. I still say you'd be smart to head back to Texas."

My face told him no.

"Your funeral," Hindman said, bringing out a big leather wallet from the inside pocket of his coat. He counted out the money in small bills. The wallet was still fat after he counted out two hundred.

"You said two-fifty a minute ago," I reminded him.

Hindman showed me the five yellow teeth left in his head. "Two hundred's enough," he said. "The other fifty's room rent. Now you take yourself over to Paddy Rainford's Fenian Hotel on Constance Street and wait till I send word on the telephone."

Hindman got up creakily from behind the desk and cranked up Central on the wall telephone and told the operator to ring him through to the Fenian Hotel. While he was waiting, Hindman showed his yellow teeth and said, "A wonderful piece of machinery, the telephone."

"Hello, Paddy," he said into the mouthpiece. Old Gordy Hindman wasn't all that much of a city slicker. Even an old shit-kicker like me knows you don't have to yell that loud over the wires.

"Hello, Paddy," he roared. "I'm sending a friend of mine over. A real nice fella. Take care of him, will you? That's right—Basso and a lot of other trouble. No, you old bastard, he ain't going to stay long. Good man, Paddy—obliged to you. That's it," Hindman said to me, coughing into his handkerchief. "Hate to be so cut and dried, but the trouble you're in could ruin a man. Our friend Basso don't exactly love me, you understand."

I finished my whiskey and took the money off Hindman's desk. Twenty years before Gordy Hindman would have faced up to Basso with nothing but his stubby hands. Now he was old and lived on oatmeal, and I understood. And if he sold me out to get cozy with the law I'd come back and break off those five yellow teeth one by one, and shove them down his turkey throat, and hold his mouth shut until he choked on them.

I wasn't sure he wouldn't sell me out. Now that he was old, maybe having his life saved wasn't such a big thing. Living on oatmeal, drooling over pictures of women he couldn't do anything about, try as he might, maybe he resented having his life saved.

"Thanks, Gordy," I said, not a bit thankful, thinking maybe I should take that fat wallet when the taking was easy. That's the kind of old friends we were, Hindman and me. "I know you're putting yourself in the way of big trouble, helping me. Just let me say thanks again."

Hindman cackled. That's the only word for the way he laughed. "Don't bust out crying, Carmody. You ain't no actor."

"Kiss my Texas ass, Gordy," I invited him.

The fit of cackling that followed that brought Hindman to death's door. When he came back from it, he told me to go out the back way.

Chapter Six

I didn't go the Paddy Rainford's hotel right away. There was a drunk with a pasty face puking his guts up in the alley behind Hindman's saloon. At another time I might have wondered why he wasn't wearing any shoes or socks.

On the way over to Constance Street, I stopped to send a telegraph message from a Western Union office that looked as if nobody had sent a message since the Yankees broke the blockade.

"Am prepared to invest money soonest needed," I wrote on the telegraph message blank. "Important discuss amount and terms income."

Doing that wore me out. I sent the message to Mr. George Verrier, St. Phail, La., and signed it Everard Mayhew, Fenian Hotel, New Orleans. I paid for a reply and told the tapper behind the desk that I'd make it worth his while to get any messages back to me right quick.

What in hell did I think I was doing? I don't

rightly know. I suppose a hunch is what it was.
To see if brother George would answer. It wasn't
much of an idea, but since I had nothing at all,
it was better than nothing.

A big man in a loud yellow coat with big
checks and green trousers was behind the desk
at the Fenian Hotel. A smaller man, older, with
a mustache so clipped it looked painted on, was
pushing papers on to a spike file. The small man
was good with the papers and the needle-pointed
spike.

Speaking to the big man, I watched the small
man and wondered why he didn't prong his girl-
ish hands with the spike.

"Pleased to make your acquainceship, Mr.
—" the big man said. He didn't say who I was.
"I'm Paddy Rainford and welcome to the Fenian Hotel. Any friend of Mr."—he left that
blank too—"is a friend of mine. I got a fine
room all picked out for you."

I didn't like him much. Big and no special age
and Irish. I don't know how big he was. Big
enough. Not taller than I was but filled out
more, lard around the middle and under the
chin. He was jumping all over himself to make
me feel at home. He even had a name picked out
for me. I guess he thought I'd write John Smith
in the register.

"Hope you enjoy your stay at the Fenian, Mr.
Rhinebeck," he said.

There was a Yankee millionaire named Rhinebeck. I guess Rainford thought he had a sense of
humor.

"The name is Everard Mayhew," I advised

him, and he had another joke ready for that
until I gave him my no-jokes look. I said there
might be a telegraph message coming in for me.
I wanted to know about it right away.

Upstairs, there was whiskey and a glass and a
bucket of ice on the dresser. The room was big,
clean enough but dusty, probably the best in the
house. The w.c. was down the hall and I decided
none of the guests could read the sign that
asked them to keep it clean.

I drank some whiskey and spilled the ice into
a towel and held it against the top of my head.
Lying on the big brass bed, I tried not to hear
the steady rattle of traffic outside on Constance
Street. I got up and pulled the finger-greased
shades and tried to sleep. Nodding off took a
while, the way things kept spinning in my head.
Chasing after Minnie Haha could be one big
waste of time. Gertie already knew who I was
when I went to her place, and she had to know
that because the police—Basso—told her. Basso
got the word from Hot Springs. A fella named
Carmody was headed for New Orleans with elev-
en thousand in his jeans. Maybe that was how
Basso worked. To get a line on moneyed citizens
running from the law. Even in a rotten town like
New Orleans he couldn't get away with taking
the money directly. He had to arrange to take it
some other way. Working with whorehouse pro-
prietors, saloon keepers and hotel operators
would be the best way to do it. The money disappeared in some kind of frame-up and the fella
who took the money in the first place was killed
off by Basso's men, or managed to get out of

town. Maybe the party to answer questions was Captain Ned Basso, not the Creole redskin Minnie.

The melting ice dripped through the towel. It felt good on my face. I dumped what was left of the ice on the floor and wiped the sweat off my face with the cold towel. If nothing happened with Minnie, if Hindman's boys couldn't find her, if they did find her and I got nothing out of her, I promised myself that I'd go after Basso. That was a laugh, with the whole police department looking for me. It sure as hell was the last thing the good captain would expect. Oh hell, I thought, it's just one big maybe . . .

I woke up, the .45 cocking itself in my hand. Whoever it was knocked again. It wasn't the police; the police wouldn't knock. Off the bed fast, I unlocked the door and got out of the way. The way the light came through the window told me I'd slept maybe two hours.

It was the agent from the telegraph office. I put the Smith & Wesson under my coat before I let him in.

"I did just what you said, Mr. Mayhew," he said. "Then after about two hours when there wasn't a reply, I sent a follow-up asking did they deliver the first message. That isn't the usual thing, but I figured it was kind of urgent, you know. I got a reply back right away. Nobody home, they said."

I gave him five dollars, and he went away.

"Always ready to be of service, Mr. Mayhew," he said. "The name is Danzig. Martin C. . . ."

I shut the door in his face and drank some

whiskey. I wondered where Minnie's brother was
off to. He wasn't just out to buy groceries; in a
place like St. Phail, a few houses and a post office, Hindman said, a telegraph message was an
event; and they'd be looking to deliver it. If
George Verrier wasn't home, most likely then he
wasn't in St. Phail. Could be he'd gone alligator
trapping or whatever in hell they did for sport in
West Louisiana. Or—another maybe—had he
decided to come to the big city to help little sis-
ter with her terrible affliction.?

Going at it again, I tried to figure what Minnie's problem could be. Maybe she was crazy.
She had seemed kind of peculiar. A girl with her
kind of good looks didn't have to work as a
whore on North Franklin Street. Maybe as some
kind of whore but not a come-one-come-all
house girl. There were lots of moneybags in the
city would be tickled to set her up in her own
place. I could see doing it myself if the money
came in steady and I stayed in one place long
enough. Minnie's affliction, so called by George,
could be that she liked to work in a whorehouse.
There were women like that; they didn't do it
for the money. There was only one thing wrong
with that kind of figuring—it didn't tie in Minnie with my eleven thousand.

There was loud whistling in the hall.
Knuckles hit the door and a man's voice called
out, "You're wanted on the telephone, sir. Did
you hear, sir?"

I said all right. The whistling went back downstairs. It didn't sound right, that whistling.
When I was a kid we whistled like that going

past Boot Hill after dark. I checked the loads in the Smith & Wesson and the Colt .38, then put them inside my belt, under the city coat.

The telephone was on the wall behind the desk. Two gents, one young, the other no special age, sat in cracked leather armchairs reading newspapers. They were reading so hard I thought they might hurt their eyes. Or maybe I was just on edge.

Rainford pointed to the telephone and smiled. The clerk followed him into his office. A voice was coming out of the telephone before I got to it. "Yeah," I said into it.

"Now listen good," Hindman was yelling at the other end of the wire.

I was listening good but not to him. I guess the two gents in the lobby should have tried to kill me sitting down. They didn't and that was a mistake. The chairs creaked when they stood up at the same time.

They had their guns out when I turned. The older gunman got off one shot before I put a third eye in his forehead. He sat down again and he was dead before his backside hit the seat. The young one tried to change his mind, but the chamber was already turning in the Smith & Wesson, and I never did hear what it was he wanted to say. The bullet tore right through his heart, but he stood there, blinking at the wonder of it all, still trying to say it was all a terrible mistake. I settled him down with a bullet in the left eye.

Maybe four seconds had been used up. After another second or two of quiet Rainford looked around the side of the half-closed door. I think he was surprised to see me on my feet. I'll say this, he looked surprised. Still and all, he was pretty quick with a comeback.

"My God, Mr. Mayhew," he said. "My God, this is terrible. Those men tried to kill you."

I put the short barrel of the .45 under his chin and dug it into the pink fat. When I took it away you could see the round mark it made. "Talk soft, Paddy," I warned him—Hindman's voice was still yelling out of the telephone— "Keep it down and maybe I'll let you live."

A man with white whiskers and red flannel long johns ran to the head of the stairs on the second floor and looked down. The face was as white as the whiskers. The gun in my hand sent him running back to his room.

Rainford started to say I was all wrong about him. To stop him I put the .45 back under his chin. The clerk didn't want to come out of the office when I told him to. I told him I'd kill him if he didn't. When he came out, I took the gun away from Rainford and cracked the clerk along the side of the head. To keep him asleep for a while was the idea; I hit him again before his knees bent enough to let him lie down.

Hindman's voice was asking for Rainford. It was loud and raspy, with fits of coughing mixed in. With the gun in Rainford's fat face, I waltzed him over to the telephone.

"Tell him what he wants to hear," I said. "Say another thing and I'll blow your spine out through your belly."

Rainford choked a bit before he got his voice

working right. Except for the old geezer in the red flannels, nobody came to ask what the shooting was all about. Constance Street sure was noisy.

'What in hell's wrong with you, Paddy?" I could hear Hindman saying. "Talk, will you, man. Is the bastard dead?"

The .45 dug into Rainford's back.

"He's dead," Rainford said. "The boys nailed him good."

More squawking came from Hindman's end.

"Sure, Corley," Rainford said. "I'll ring the police and tell them what happened. "Sure, Corley, the cowboy tried to rob . . . That's it, sure. Me and Benny were too quick for him and . . . That's good, Corley, I'll tell the boys to get back right away."

Hindman's voice said he was obliged to Rainford for his cooperation. There was a click. Rainford didn't know what to do. He stayed there with his fat mouth pushed up against the telephone. A belt across the kidneys reminded him that the conversation was over.

"Rip the telephone off the wall," I ordered him. I guess he wasn't thinking straight, because he didn't do it. Another bang in the kidneys woke him up and made him try. Fear had turned his muscles to jelly and the telephone didn't budge. I could have done it myself with one hand. Mean was the way I felt; I wanted him to do it.

"Try harder, Paddy," I said. "Because the next thing hits you is a bullet."

"Good man," I praised him when the flabby

bastard got that telephone dismantled. It looked like there wasn't a man, black or white, I could count on in the whole city of New Orleans. I didn't have to hit Rainford after he wrecked the telephone. Sure, I took the bad feeling out on him. I hit him, and it made me feel better. I hit him again, and then I got tired of it. The next time I hit him was business, to keep him from getting word back to Hindman that I was still alive. The way he lay, it looked as if he might never wake up, and I wasn't one bit sorry for that.

I got over to Claffey Street fast. It didn't take more than five minutes, and I went around through the alley to Hindman's back door. Hindman would be expecting his two killers about now. I didn't even have to pull a bluff: Hindman opened the door on the first knock.

Gordy's old-man mouth began to dribble when he saw the gun and the man behind it.

"That wasn't friendly, Gordy," I told him, waving him backward with the gun. "It wasn't nice, and it wasn't friendly. And it wasn't smart."

Hindman went back behind the desk and sat down, and I didn't tell him not to. There would be some kind of gun in the desk, but Hindman was too old to try for it.

The old bastard tried on a grin. "It was smart enough," he said. "Only it didn't work out. Well, so be it, as the fella said."

Next he tried the soft soap. "Should of knowed I couldn't get the better of you, Carmody. I always did say you . . ."

"You should have listened to yourself," I said. "I mean, when you said I was too fast to be double-crossed by an old man and back-shot by city trash. But we'll let that go for a while. Where's Minnie?"

"Can we deal, Carmody?"

I said I might let him live if he told me. He knew it was the best offer he was likely to get.

"She's holed up in a hotel at the foot of Poydras Street, near the river," Hindman said. "The Hotel Garreau. Registered in the name of Elizabeth Delgado. That's the gospel truth, Carmody."

"That better be so, Gordy. You steer me wrong and I'll be back. You know that."

Hindman looked surprised. "You mean you ain't going to kill me?"

I nodded.

Hindman mopped his mouth. "Well, then, I'd better tell the truth. The whore's at a hotel on Girod Street. Registered as Catherine Marais. The name of the hotel is the La Hache."

I didn't know what to make of the old bastard. He was so crooked, I figured they'd have to screw him into the ground when he died—which might not be too far in the future, the way he was going. I told him to forget the eleven thousand. I said it wasn't worth it. Not the way I'd kill him if he crossed me again.

I went out the way I came in. Basso was going in the front door when I stepped out of the alley on to Claffey Street. Basso's hard hat rode high on his bullet head; a thin line of bandage showed under the hat brim. The Captain was in right bad humor; a drunk got in his way and was knocked, puking, into the gutter. The way he hit the swinging doors threatened to knock them off the hinges.

I had to move fast. A kid was going by in a spring wagon. "Hang on, mister," he said when I waved a five dollar bill in his face and let him take it. He whipped up the horse and headed down Jackson Avenue toward the waterfront. The light delivery wagon bounced all over the cobblestones on the docks and with my weight I didn't sit as light as the kid.

The Hotel La Hache looked to be a hundred years old. About the same number of years had gone by since the paint on it was new. Two wooden buttresses were doing their best to keep the front wall from falling into the street. At least some of the windows on all four floors were broken and the ones with rags stuffed in the holes were the better rooms, I decided. I had seen worse looking rattraps than the Hotel La Hache, but I couldn't remember them offhand.

The fat man behind the desk was a Mexican or a Cuban, something like that. He looked dead, but he was only dead drunk. He filled the swivel chair he was in like an egg in an eggcup. Or maybe like jelly in a bowl, because some of the fat oozed over the arms of the chair. The smell he gave off wasn't quite as bad as a dead horse left for a week in the sun.

"Miss Marais' room," I said. "Wake up, Pancho."

A gold tooth made a dull glint in his dirty

mouth. "Pancho?" he said, spreading his fat hands, palms up. "Is no Pancho here, gringo."

In maybe another five minutes Basso would be knocking down the front door of the Hotel La Hache. There was no one else in the smelly lobby. I took out the Smith & Wesson and cocked it. "It's a real gun," I told the fat man.

"Room Nine, second floor," he said, polite as only a scared fat man can be polite when he wants to be.

"Is she there now?" I asked.

The fat man showed me his palms again. "Who can say?" he said. "Sometimes I sleep."

"More sleep is what you need," I said, going around behind the desk. I don't know why he thought I wanted to kill him. But he did, and he tried to get his fat carcass out of the chair. I hit him where his neck bulged out behind. There was so much fat, I had to hit him again before his eyes closed and the fat bulk sagged back into the chair. I guess he was comfortable enough; he began to snore.

The bottle he was drinking from was under the desk, still half full of tequila. After I wiped it off good, I took a drink and spilled what was left over the fat man's shirt. I stuck the empty bottle between his thick legs and left it there.

A door behind the desk opened into a small room full of broken furniture. Boards were nailed over the window, and it was dark. With the door halfway open I waited for Basso.

Chapter Seven

A little man with a leather cap stuck on the back of his head came down the stairs and went out. The spring bell on the door was still jingling when Basso walked in. When Basso walked in anywhere the floor shook under his two hundred and fifty pounds, and he looked more like a bull than a man. A bull in a loud suit walking on its hind legs. The biggest and toughest bull in New Orleans.

There was an old punch bell on the desk. Basso didn't use it. He kicked the front of the desk with his double-soled boots. I could imagine some of the other things Basso kicked with those boots. When all the yelling didn't wake up the clerk, Basso went behind the desk and rocked the fat man's head with some pretty good slaps.

I wanted to be sure. I didn't tell Basso to put his hands up until he turned his back, and he sure as hell didn't want to do it. I couldn't see the red in his face, but the color ran around the sides of his bull's neck.

"Put your right hand behind your head, then drop your gun with the other hand," I told him. "Don't hurry—nice and slow. Then take off that coat and drop it. After that turn around all the way. Then take two giant steps toward the stairs."

It looked like this was my day for short-barreled Smith & Wessons. Basso carried it in a shoulder holster, and there were no other guns in sight when he took off the coat. His meaty face wasn't just red when he turned around; it was close to purple. I guess it was kind of hard on him, the meanest bull in New Orleans, being taken twice in the same day, by the same man.

Putting the boots to any kind of lawman is one thing I like to do. "We keep this up, chief, you're going to run out of guns. I sure hope you don't have to pay for them yourself."

The red stayed in Basso's face, but his eyes were cold, his voice, too. "You better kill me now, Carmody," he said. "Because if you don't I'm going to rip out your guts."

"I'll bet you say that to all the boys," I said. "You think the whole world wets its pants when you walk by. Maybe you're pretty good beating up sneak thieves and sick whores. Now me, I think you're just a thief who doesn't have the guts to do it out in the open. Like the rest of us thieves."

I didn't expect Basso to grin. "That's because I'm smarter than you are," he said. "You aren't smart at all, cowboy. Or you'd be long gone from New Orleans."

I grinned back at him. "Let's go on up to Minnie's room, and we'll talk some more. Start climbing those stairs."

I kept well away from Basso. He didn't like it when I wouldn't let him get out of the way after he knocked on the door. Nobody shot through the door, and I told Basso to break it down. One kick from the double-soled boots did the trick.

The room was dark and hot and the man lying on the floor with a knife in his chest wasn't making any noise. The window shade wouldn't go up. Basso ripped it down, scattering dust. Basso felt the side of the dead man's neck and straightened up.

"How long?" I asked him.

"Hard to say, maybe an hour. Did you do it?"

"Come on, Basso."

"All right," Basso said. "I guess you didn't do it."

"And I didn't kill Gertie."

Basso looked at me. "That's what you keep saying. If you didn't, then who did?"

"Maybe you did, Basso. You knew about me the minute I hit town. Got a telegram from Hot Springs describing me. Knew about the eleven thousand. Tipped off Gertie and got me robbed. Then you double-crossed Gertie, killed her or had her killed, and rigged it so the mountain would fall on me."

"You ought to be a detective," Basso said. "A detective in the Ladies Auxiliary."

I kept the gun on him while he went through

the dead man's pockets. I knew it was George Verrier before Basso found a wallet and said that's who it was. The face was dark, like Minnie's, and the features were the same. George was wearing an old-fashioned ruffled shirt of the kind you hardly ever see any more. It hadn't been washed lately, and the cuffs were frayed.

"You know who he is?" Basso asked.

"You're off duty right now, officer. I'll ask the questions."

Basso paid no mind to that. Acting tough was a habit hard to break. "For Christ's sake, cowboy, do you know him or not."

"Maybe," I said. "No reason to tell you."

I didn't know whether to believe Basso when he said, "Maybe you didn't kill Gertie. And, for Christ's sake, don't keep saying I did."

I asked him why not.

Now Basso was hedging again. "Because if you killed Gertie, there was no reason not to kill me when you had the chance. They couldn't hang you but once."

"Not good enough, Basso. Maybe that explains why I didn't kill her. But what about you?"

Basso gave up trying to fool me. Least I think he did. "No reason for me to kill Gertie," he said. "None at all. I own Gertie's—she just worked for me. We got along fine. I get along fine with everybody. A lot of people all over town work for me. We get along fine. That's the way business should be, profitable and peaceful. No holding out, no double-dealing. Why, man, I get a cut of just about everything but the Sunday collections. I let that go; I'm not greedy. Why in hell should I risk everything to get a lousy eleven thousand dollars?"

"I don't know," I said. "It sounds sensible enough the way you tell it. Supposing you're out of it—what about Gertie? Maybe she got tired of working for wages?"

Basso moved his strong brown teeth like grindstones. He was impatient, or acting that way. "Gertie worked for me for close to eleven years. She got a percentage of the take and never pulled down less than two thousand a month. Gertie was worth more than you stole in your whole life."

"Maybe so," I said. "What happens now?"

Basso took his hands down. I told him to put them back where they were. I asked him the same question.

"Nobody messes with Ned Basso," he said. "That goes for you too, cowboy."

I sure as hell was messing with him, but I didn't press the point.

Basso said, "It took me fifteen years to get this town the way I want it. I run things my way, and when I say something I make it stick. Everybody's got their hand out—the Mayor, the City Council, the Chief of Police. They got their business interests, and I got mine. Gertie was one of them, and I aim to do something about it. If I don't the whole thing could fall to pieces."

"Which makes you an honest crook," I said. "Business as usual is what you want?"

Basso grinned. "Somebody's got to pay for Gertie," he said. "You would have done fine."

"You think Minnie Haha did it?" I asked him. "She did run away. And now there's her brother."

"What brother?"

"The dead man on the floor."

"Oh," said Basso. "On the floor."

"Not on the ceiling, officer."

"You got a big mouth, cowboy," Basso said. "Someday it's going to get you in a lot of trouble."

I was thinking. "How did Gertie know who I was?"

"Because I told her," Basso answered. "On the telephone. I had a man watching you from the minute you got into town. He telephoned me and said you'd gone into Gertie's place. I telephoned Gertie and told her you were a bad lad from out West. To knock you on the head—to kill you, if that didn't work. I mean, if you tried to burn the place."

On the face of it, Basso's story made some sense. Looking at him it was easy to believe he had a heavy interest in every dirty business in New Orleans. Of course, he'd listened to so many smooth stories in his time that making one up for me would be no trouble at all.

Basso said, "I know what you're thinking, Carmody. "You're thinking you could ruin me with what I just told you. Don't you believe it. What could you do—tell the Chief of Police? I got enough on the chief to hang him—and not just in a manner of speaking. Now you want to deal with me or not?"

"Answer this first," I told him. "I crippled a

city detective, killed the black and two of Corley Harkins' gunmen in the Fenian Hotel. All in self defense, naturally. Where does that leave me, even if I didn't kill Gertie?"

"Shooting that detective was bad business, Carmody. I guess he'll be all right. The others—well, I'd say we can file it under Miscellaneous. Soon as the Gertie killing is cleared up you can get the hell out of my town."

"With my eleven thousand," I reminded him.

Basso was all crook. He grinned. "Filing things under Miscellaneous costs money, cowboy. Fifty-five hundred, to be exact about it. That's the deal. The only one in town."

It was something to think about. There was only one thing that said maybe I should deal with Basso. Like him or not, and I didn't, the man looked like a professional. A professional lawman and a professional crook. Most of the time you can't trust lawmen with sticky fingers. In a pinch some of them turn out to be more lawman than thief. Or they get scared and try to double back and prove they were true-blue fellas after all.

Basso wasn't like that. He wasn't just a crooked bull; he was a businessman. I like to do business with a man who knows his business and wants to protect it.

"Here's your gun back," I said, tossing the second Smith & Wesson his way. He caught it easily with his left hand. Looking at me, he checked the loads and spun the chamber. He hefted the short-barreled .45, looking to see how

I took it. Finally, the gun went into the shoulder holster.

"Okay," he said. "First you talk. Don't hold back, cowboy. It wastes time. You want that money, and I want you gone from New Orleans. What about this dead man?"

I told him about the letters I found in Minnie's dresser. I said that George there on the floor was having trouble keeping his head above swamp water. Kept asking if Minnie could send money to save the family honor. And he wasn't at home to receive my telegraph message.

"You think Minnie and George killed Gertie?" I asked Basso. "George was in town on some kind of business. Could be that Minnie saw a clear chance to get hold of some big money. Enough to send the tax collector packing. The guard at the hotel did say a man and a woman opened my strongbox."

Basso took off his hard hat, touched his bandaged head, gave me a mean look, and put the hat on again. It was kind of embarrassing to see the bandages. Basso said, "The guard said a young woman and a big heavyset man probably older. George here looks about twenty-four. Not tall and thin as a rail. Anyway, how would Minnie know about the eleven thousand?"

"Maybe Gertie told her," I suggested.

Basso shook his head. "Not Gertie. Gertie never gets friendly with the girls."

I had a thought. "Would she tell Sam Nails? Would she have?"

"It's possible," Basso said slowly, eyeing me hard and not just because of the hurt in his head. "Yes, sir, it's possible she did. That buck's been with her a long time. As long as I knew her. Longer than that, I'd say. Got him out of the Parish Prison. Something like that, the best I remember."

"Well?" I said.

"That's all wet, Carmody. The nigger didn't do it. Gertie was good to that boy."

"And they say Abe Lincoln liked actors."

Basso got up and walked around, and he had to step over the dead man to do it. Every time he turned his back on me I got ready to shoot him. But Basso was the kind of man who did one thing at a time. He was thinking now; maybe he'd try to kill me later. He stepped back over the dead man and put his wide backside on the edge of the bed.

"It's still all wet," he said, not as sure as the words meant to be. "Now if Gertie was twenty years younger and it was rape along with murder—sure it could be the nigger. And even that won't wash. You ever hear of a houseman in a cathouse having to rape anybody? Gertie had plenty of colored girls for customers liked dark meat."

I thought this new team of detectives, Carmody & Basso, was taking too long to come to the point. Any kind of point. "What's all this bullshit about rape? Why couldn't Samuel J. Nails decide to snag that eleven thousand for himself? The big bastard was smart. I know that and don't tell me he wasn't. Gertie could have told him—you said so yourself. They'd been together a long time, and she could have mentioned it.

The way you see it, she was good to Nails. Gertie saw it that way, too. But what about Nails himself?"

Basso said, "The nigger always looked okay to me. He had money in the bank. Some money. Not a lot. Enough for a nigger. I checked on him myself a while back. I tell you, the nigger was doing fine."

I wasn't one bit sure that Nails killed Gertie. I said to Basso, "What were you doing when you were forty?"

Basso didn't put anything together, but he answered. "The same as now," he said. "Chief of Detectives."

"You weren't a forty-year-old towel boy and bouncer in a whorehouse. That's what Nails was. Nails was forty, give or take some."

"For Christ's sake, Carmody, where you from anyway? Nails was a nigger!"

I started to put a smoke together. Basso said he didn't want one. Didn't smoke *or* drink. I began to wish I hadn't given back his gun. "All right," I said. "You're the detective."

Basso took out a toothpick and chewed on it. It was a gold toothpick attached to his watch chain by another smaller chain. He snapped at the gold toothpick like a dog on a rat hunt.

I waited.

Finally, he said, "Could be. You never know in this job. Times change—maybe. The nigger could have done it. You were out cold, first in the whore's bed."

Basso put a mean grin on his face. "You were

out, not able to do a thing. I guess you aren't so tough."

No answer was called for.

"Then the nigger carried you to that other room where you woke up. You slept there most of the night. That gave the nigger all the time he needed to kill Gertie, before or after the money was taken from the strongbox. The shot-gun guard said he didn't get a clear look at the man who came in with the woman. Just he was big, older than the woman, and with a big hat down over his face."

"Minnie?" I asked

"Sure looks that way, Carmody. She was there and the nigger was there. Gertie, say, told the nigger about the money, about you. What bothers me is why this woman, whore or not, would team up with a nigger? The nigger was doing all right for himself and the whore, the way you tell it, wasn't interested in a god-damned thing. Just lay there like a dog in a basket. Why would they all of a sudden up and kill Gertie and rob you?"

"Gertie was handy—that's all. What they really wanted was the money. I was handy, too. They figured—somebody figured—how to take the money and sic the whole New Orleans Police Department on poor old Carmody. The law would kill me or catch me or I'd run back to Texas and keep going. The law would have me down on the books for a killing and they'd have the money. Only they robbed and framed the wrong man."

His feet clear of the floor, Basso tapped the

dead man in the side of the head with his boot. Nothing mean was in the way he did it. Basso had seen a lot of dead men on dirty floors. The Chief of Detectives was thinking hard. He tapped while he thought, and not being dead long enough to stiffen up, George Verrier's head rolled a bit.

"Why would she kill her own brother?" Basso wanted to know. "That is, if he is her brother, and she is mixed up in this, and if she did kill him. What about that, Detective Carmody? I know, I know. George here wanted some kind of share of the money, and the whore killed him. Her own brother."

"I don't know," I said.

Basso stood up and groaned. "We're not doing any good holding a wake over this dead meat."

"What's the plan?" I enquired.

"Plan!" Basso was fed up. "The plan, cowboy, is to get the hell out of here."

Chapter Eight

We went back downstairs after Basso made a worse wreck of the room than it was. Nothing turned up. Nothing in the drawers of the rickety dresser, no sign even that the bed had been slept in. Except for his name and that he was dead, George Verrier had no more information to give.

The Hotel La Hache didn't have a telephone. Basso broke some more furniture trying to find one. He started slapping the unconscious fat man, and I had to explain why he was sleeping so sound.

Basso's temper came and went all the time. Now it went. "I'll wake the greaser," he said. He found a bottle of tequila under the desk and knocked off the neck. I didn't have time to ask him to save some for me before he dumped it over the fat man's head, broken glass and all.

When the smell reached his hairy nose, the fat man began to mutter. "That's the boy," Basso said encouragingly. "Open those big brown eyes, you filthy bastard."

Reaching down, Basso pinched the inside of the fat man's thigh, a painful place. The fat face quivered. Basso did it again. There was a yelp, and the fat man woke up. He gave out with some long Spanish curses. He doubled his fat fists, and Basso backhanded him across the face.

It was not a good day for that tacos eater, and he knew it for sure when he saw who was doing the slapping. I could understand why he closed his eyes and tried to go back to sleep.

Basso knew how to keep him awake and interested. It's hard not to notice when somebody is doing his damnedest to break your thumb. Letting up on the thumb, Basso hit him again.

A trickle of blood ran down the fat man's chin, but the smile he gave Basso was beautiful. Like a reject from the poor farm trying to butter up his hard-hearted kinfolk. When he looked past Basso and saw me, he started to holler bloody murder. "Arrest this man, captain. He try to kill me!"

Basso made a fist and got ready to deliver it. The hollering was turned off like water from a spigot. He smiled at Basso's fist. I guess smiling came easy for him.

"The girl upstairs," Basso started, not lowering the fist. "Let's hear every little thing you know, Pancho." The Mexican didn't object to being called Pancho, not by Basso. "When she checked in. When she checked out. The visitors she had. The way everybody looked and what they said. You know the routine, Pancho."

A dribble of tequila was left in the broken bottle, and Pancho asked if he could have it. Basso said he could have it in the face.

Pancho hurried up. "She check in about noontime, captain. By herself. No bag. No nothing. I make her pay in cash in advance."

The Mexican smiled. "I think it kind of funny she had no bag."

"I'll bet you did," Basso commented.

"The man come to see her couple of hour later," the Mexican went on. "Nice looking young friend of th lady, he say. I think it's okay and let him go up. I don't know what happen after that. I guess I get tired and take a siesta. I don't seen nobody go in or out. Not till this gringo show up."

Basso slapped him.

"Be polite, Pancho," he said. "Always be polite when you're talking to me."

Pancho never ran out of smiles. "Sure, captain. For you I'm all the time polite."

Basso took his solid backside away from the edge of the desk. He hooked his thumbs through the armholes of his vest and drummed his fingers on his chest. The gold Chief of Detectives badge was pinned to the vest, over his heart. The badge meant a lot to the Mexican. He kept looking at it.

"You sure that's all, Pancho?" Basso asked in that slow dead voice. "Try to be sure before you answer."

"Sure I'm sure," the Mexican said.

"You're really sure?" Basso asked again. "Because that nice young fella is lying upstairs with a knife in his chest. I'd hate to hang you for that."

This time Pancho had to work to produce a smile. He rubbed the back of his neck where my gun had bounced off the muscle. "Honest, Captain," he said. "A stack of Bibles, I have no part in this. I sleep like I say. I tell you everything."

"Except how many times the woman was here before," Basso said. "How many times was that? And who with?" She ever come here with a nigger, Pancho?"

The Mexican looked sick. "You know I don't run that kinda place, captain. Not a flop for no niggers. You beat me all you want, and I still say no nigger come here with a white lady. I do a lot of stuff, but I don't do that. Beat me—I still say the same."

Basso put his hands in his pockets and jingled some coins. "Beat you, old pal? After all the years we been having these little visits? Why, Pancho, don't you know I *like* Mexicans."

I had seen many the mean bastard do his stuff, but Basso was a real expert. The city trash he dealt with never knew what he was going to do next. The Mexican knew Basso better than most, I guess. He got set to take another belt in the face. And he got it.

Now that he'd used up his bad feeling on the Mexican, Basso was in good humor again. "Sorry for the rough stuff, Pancho. You know how it is."

"That's okay," the Mexican said.

I followed Basso out into the street.

"We got to find a telephone," he said, all business now, a real badge-toter.

It didn't look like he'd pried loose much information from the Mexican. I said so.

"The nigger was there all right," Basso told me. "Not today—we know that—but other times. How many times doesn't count. The thing is, he was there with the woman. Pancho was scared to admit it. Even in New Orleans renting rooms to buck niggers and white women could get him lynched. I could beat it out of him if there was time. No point in that. Didn't you see the greaser's face when I asked him? The whore and the nigger used the hotel. I guess they had to pay plenty."

Basso was so pleased with himself he began to whistle. Where we were was the bad end of Girod Street, where it runs into the river, and the drunks and the pickpockets and the rat-faced pimps got out of Basso's way when they saw him coming.

"Why aren't you in jail, Mikey?" he yelled at a one-eyed weasel in a cloth cap.

"Just got out, captain," Mikey answered, stepping off the sidewalk. "Couldn't spare a handout, could you?"

Basso dug out two-bits and flipped it into the middle of the street. The one-eyed man ran after it, blessing Basso and all his descendants.

"You should have been a detective, Carmody," Basso said. "It's a fine dirty life."

A big brassy saloon made a lot of noise down the street. The name of it was Big Bill Gately's Bar & Restaurant. A powerful smell of pickled pig's feet came out into the street and, I guess, that took care of the restaurant end.

With me behind him, Basso walked in like he owned the place. That was the way he walked and talked, and it seemed to work most of the time. The man behind the bar saw Basso and tried to make a run for the back room. Basso was quick for his size. He grabbed a beer mug off a table inside the door and used it to break the big mirror behind the bar.

The bartender stopped running and turned around. He wasn't half as good at smiling as the Mexican. But he did say, "Nice to see you, captain."

Basso was still in good humor. "Just want to borrow your telephone, Jimmy. Where would that be?"

While the bartender was telling Basso where it was, Big Bill Gately, who was more big-bellied than big, came out of his office. Gately was wearing a yellow-check suit and a sour look. Having his mirror smashed didn't go down too well with him. An old bare-knuckles prize fighter was what he looked like—the lumpy scars over the eyes, the thick ears, and flat nose. I guess he still thought he was pretty tough.

"There was no call for that, Basso," he said in a Yankee accent.

Basso smiled at him "Now you know that's not true, Big Bill. Anything I do is called for. And you know why? Because I feel like it. Wouldn't you say that's a fact?"

Big Bill didn't want to back down. After a

while, still sour-faced, he did. Yeah, he said, what Basso said was a fact.

We went into Gately's office. Basso told Gately to go and water the whiskey. While he was waiting for Central to ring him through to police headquarters, I stuck my head out the door and told the bartender to fetch some whiskey. Gately had gone to sit with some poker players. The man brought the whiskey and said it was on the house. I had the feeling it would be.

"Hello, Frank," Basso said into the telephone. "Yeah, Basso. Wait a minute, Frank."

Basso told me to close the door.

"Fine, Frank," Basso said. "What I want you to do. Check the files and see what we got on a nigger name of Samuel J. Nails. Did a stretch in the Parish Prison a long time ago. You'll have to dig back some. While you're at it, check on a whore goes by the name of Minnie Haha. Yeah, Frank, just like the poem only this is two words."

Basso spelled the goddamned silly name. "The real name is Frances Verrier. You won't find anything. Check it anyway. Do it right away. I'll wait."

I finished the first drink of whiskey and looked at Basso. He was having one hell of a good time. He said if the whiskey wasn't good he'd kick Gately's Yankee ass back to Boston.

"Look, Basso," I said. "You don't have to put on a show for me. I'm convinced. You're a big man in New Orleans and tough as a mule steak. A mosquito bites you—he dies. Fair enough?"

Basso rubbed his wide belly with both hands.

"Maybe I was overdoing it," he agreed. "I just wanted you to be sure of your man. Nobody ever outsmarted Ned Basso."

"Fine," I told him. "The same goes for me."

"By Christ, you're all right, Carmody. You ought to be working for me. With a man like you to back me up I could own this town."

I said I thought he did.

A whistle came out of the telephone. "Yeah, Frank," Basso said, listening while the other bull at headquarters said his piece.

I drank some more whiskey.

"That's all on the nigger and nothing on the whore. Neither name. Right, Frank, I got it," Basso said.

"Let's go," he said to me.

On the way out, Gately came over and asked Basso if there was anything else he could do. Whiskey had put some courage back in the old prize fighter's flabby frame.

"Give me regards to your lovely wife," Basso said.

Gately looked offended. "My wife's dead."

"That's Nature's way of telling her to slow down," Basso said, in better form than ever.

Outside, I asked Basso where in hell we were going.

The big bull rubbed his hands together like a kid about to attack an apple pie.

"Check your gun, Carmody," he said. "You and me are going to Niggertown."

My gun was checked enough. Basso checked his.

The thought crossed my mind that Captain

Ned Basso was more than a little crazy. You know what he said? He said, "This way to the fireworks."

But that was all right. I felt a little crazy myself

Chapter Nine

We walked up from the river to the nearest
trolley line. Basso stood out on the tracks and
stopped the first horsecar to come along. "Right
to the end of the line—no stops, Mac," he told
the driver. "Official business, get her moving."

The trolley operator knew Basso and wasn't
about to argue. "Everybody off, folks," Basso
yelled at the riders. "No back talk—get the hell
off."

An old French gent with a spike beard shook
his stick at Basso—at me, too. Basso told him
something in pig French. He climbed down
quick enough after that.

It was getting dark outside, and the dirty
streets looked better with the lights coming on.
The driver laid the whip on the animals, and the
car rolled along the street tracks about as fast as
a man can run. The signs said we were on Ramparts Street.

Basso rested his big feet on another seat and

rubbed the insteps, groaning as he did it. "It's true about policemen's feet," he informed me. "You want to hear something interesting?" he asked me, dragging it out from habit, always trying to needle the other fella. "You know where the nigger was from originally? From the same town as your sweetheart—St. Phail. The arrest file didn't say what he did there, but that's where he's from. Born there in 1854. That would make him thirty-seven or -eight. Arrested here in '74 and did two years in jail for maiming another nigger. After that he worked for Gertie."

"You're right," I said. "That is interesting."

"Frank says the nigger's father is still alive. Least he was the last time they brought the files up to date. Frank says the old dinge runs some kind of Voodoo church on St. Ann Street. That's over by Congo Square and that's where we're going. Could be we'll find the girl or the money. Or both."

I chewed on that for a while. Life in New Orleans sure was complicated, at least for me. I guess a man like Basso liked it that way. Now me, I can do without all that brainwork. A man tries to kill me, and I try to stop him. That's complicated enough for me. I had to smile at the next thought I had. Next time I took some big money maybe I'd put it in a bank for safekeeping.

Basso stood up. "Now we walk," he said. Needling me again, he said, "Could be you'll have a chance to show how fast you are with a gun.

They got niggers down here make your Texas killers look like old ladies."

Off Ramparts Street the streets got dark and narrow, and the stink would take twenty minutes to explain. The sewer system in New Orleans never was anything for the city fathers to brag about; down here in the colored section it didn't exist at all. There were still some weeks to go before the real bad summer heat set in, but it was kind of hard to imagine how much worse this part of the city could smell when it did.

"Walk in the middle of the street or you'll get a bath," Basso warned me. A mechanical piano was knocking its brains out trying to play a quick-step and sure enough, just like Basso said, a third floor window slammed up and a pisspot emptied into the street.

Basso got spots on his boots; it didn't bother him. "We call that nigger artillery," he said. "The women are better shots than the men."

A cluster of colored men were throwing dice on the sidewalk. The only light came from a short candle in a broken bottle. They were making a lot of noise, but none of it made sense to me. One of them stood up when they heard us coming: a big yellow gent with gold earrings and a red rag tied around his head. He was the first man I'd seen in New Orleans who didn't seem to be afraid of Basso.

"How do, Xavier," Basso said easily. "Nice night."

The yellow man was very polite in a French accent. It was funny to hear the polite voice coming out of such a mean looking bastard. The men crouched around the candle didn't move. "Yes, a most pleasant night," the rag-head said. "Perhaps rain later most probably."

"Well, goodnight," Basso said.

"Goodnight, captain," Xavier answered.

The dice started rattling again, and we turned into St. Ann Street. Basso was looking for No. 25. Even in the dim light it wasn't hard to find. A low two-story house painted a bright blue, with pictures of men and animals, and devils, I guess, painted over the blue in other colors. Iron shutters covered the windows and the door was faced with heavy tin. The shutters were red, the door another kind of blue.

People were singing or chanting inside and they stopped even before Basso rattled the door with his big fist. The house might have been closed up for fifty years—not a sound. Basso opened his coat and loosened the Smith & Wesson in the shoulder holster. "Watch it," he said to me. "I wasn't fooling back there."

I expected Basso to start kicking the door. He didn't. "Doctor Jack," he called, loud and tough but still respectful.

"You got to humor these Voodoo niggers," he explained, keeping his voice low.

"Open up, Doctor Jack," he said. "Chief of Detectives Basso. Don't you be foolish now, Doctor Jack. I just want to talk with you."

"Go away," a slow deep voice said through the door. "You disturbing the house of worship. They ain't no gals whiskey neither in here. Go along or you be sorry. Doctor Jack have spoken."

Basso's store of good humor was running out. It didn't take much to turn him sour. The only noise came from his strong brown teeth grinding together. It was too dark to see the dark red in his face, but it was there. In another minute, if the Reverend Doctor didn't open the door, Basso's temper would explode like a busted boiler.

I heard a small noise at the end of the street and when I looked I thought I saw the yellow man with the gold earrings. "You'd better open up, Doctor Jack," Basso was saying. "There will be bad trouble if you don't. Captain Basso have spoken."

I had to grin at that; the meanness in Basso always came out.

"Black bastard," he growled.

"Watch it," I said. "He'll put a curse on you."

A heavy bolt rattled in its slot. Altogether, four dead-bolts were shot before the door opened. The man who opened it was black as a wet crow and the powerful shoulders looked too heavy for his runty legs to hold up. He looked like a big man who'd been shortened by about a foot. One thing he wasn't, and that was scared. Basso didn't tell him it was a nice night, so I guess here was one citizen of New Orleans he didn't know.

With the door half open I could see candles burning inside and a funny smell, thick and sweet, drifted out into my face. Basso stiff-armed the door, but the black had his shoulder behind it.

"You got to show something proves police,"

the doorkeeper demanded. "White folks come saying police, that don't prove they is."

Basso flipped his coat open and showed the badge pinned to his vest. The Lord's Prayer might have been engraved there; it took the black about that long tc make out what the badge said.

"Satisfied?" Basso wanted to know.

"Anybody can own a badge," the black started.

Suddenly Basso's voice got cold and dead. "Move out of the way, pal. Or I'll move you."

After we got inside, I began to think we'd have done better to stay in the street. The room was long and low and full of blacks, maybe twenty-five or thirty, still on their knees in front of some kind of wooden altar, all the heads turned our way. The four bolts slammed home again and I haven't had such a closed-in feeling since I fell down a dry well as a kid.

Picking out Doctor Jack was easy even without the medicine man outfit he had draped around his shoulders. The Reverend was Sam Nails with twenty years added to his age, with all his hair gone, and no teeth. The difference was, the meanness in Sam Nails didn't show much in his face; the old man looked vicious enough to bite himself. Sixty some years had slowed him up, but his eyes were as bright and quick as a snake's. I couldn't think of any work he was better suited for than putting curses on people.

"Are you John Nails?" Basso asked him, taking no heed of the hostile black faces.

Doctor Jack held up his hands and there was blood on them, on the sleeves of his robe, at the corners of his toothless mouth. Something flapped weakly on the wooden altar behind him—a dying chicken. Well now, I thought, the old boy's been drinking chicken blood.

"There is no John Nails here," he informed Basso. "That is a slave name. My name is Doctor Jack. I tell you nothing."

Basso clenched his fists but kept them at his sides. The bulge at the back of his neck was turning red. "I haven't asked you anything yet, your reverence. Now suppose we drop the bullshit. Just answer the questions and we'll get along fine."

An angry sound ran through Doctor Jack's congregation. The doorkeeper was behind me, and I figured he'd have to die before it was safe to start shooting at the others. I was ready to bet there wasn't a man in the room who didn't have a razor or a knife on him. No matter how fast we pulled the trigger, it wouldn't make any difference.

"Tell those boys to settle down," Basso said to Doctor Jack. "The first man moves, you get sent to Voodoo heaven. I'm not going to tell you again."

"What do you want?" Doctor Jack asked. His eyes were trying hard to turn us into bullfrogs.

Basso's hands unclenched. He made a powerful effort to sound sympathetic, but that was one thing Basso couldn't manage. "I came to tell you your son Samuel is dead. He was killed this

morning. I knew him well, Doctor Jack," Basso
lied. "A hell of a nice boy."

Doctor Jack's snaky eyes stayed bright and
cold. Like a snake, he didn't blink, and even in
the hot stinking room his black skin was dry and
dead looking, with no shine to it. He looked at
Basso, then at me. The old black face was like
one of those devil masks the Mexican Indians
make to scare themselves. The slow deep voice
dragged itself up from his chest. He said:

"My son was murdered by a white man—Carmody. My son was not a fine boy. He was a nigger pimp for the white folks. They use him as a
pimp, then they kill him. You are not looking for
Carmody. Not in this place."

"I'm looking for some money," Basso said.
"Eleven thousand dollars. The money and the
woman who has it. Who stole it from your son
after she killed him. Never mind about this Carmody. Carmody was nowhere near the whorehouse when your son was killed. I'm telling you
the woman did it. She got your son mixed up in
a murder, then she killed him, and blamed both
murders on this Carmody. She wanted all the
money for herself."

Doctor Jack stood there like a rock, the
blood-stained hands folded against his chest.
The congregation was as quiet and still as the
reverend himself. Basso had left a space for Doctor Jack to chew on what he'd said. To say
something himself, if he had a mind to. Doctor
Jack didn't move, didn't speak.

"What I'm telling you is the truth," Basso
lied. "If you don't believe me, you can come

down to headquarters and read the report for yourself." Basso didn't ask the reverend if he could read. "Your son lived long enough to make a full confession," Basso went on with his yarn. "How this woman double-crossed him, shot him down like a dog."

Doctor Jack spoke. "Why would the woman come here?"

"Because you were Samuel's father. Because you might help her. Your son was jocking this woman, Doctor Jack. You knew he was dead— everybody in New Orleans knows it by now— but you couldn't have known about the dying confession. We kept quiet about that, hoping the woman would think she was in the clear. Sure she ran but that's because she lost her nerve. We hope she'll get it back. The way I figure it, she came to you for help. Maybe offered you some money."

So far, Basso had been dodging around. Suddenly, he came to the point. "Where's the woman, uncle? And where's the money? Talk straight, and we'll forget your part in this. The charge is murder and robbery. Start leading me in circles and I'll help to hang you myself, you goddamned cannibal."

Basso had tried the easy way, and it didn't work. Now it was a showdown, and I was part of it. Doctor Jack moved his right hand, and everybody got up off their knees. Basso didn't grab for his gun. He took it out and held it by his side. I did the same.

Basso raised the Smith & Wesson like a shooter aiming at a target. I moved away from the squat doorkeeper, and he didn't follow me. Basso's .45 was pointing straight at Doctor Jack's heart. "I asked you a question," he said. "And you got thirty seconds to answer it."

Doctor Jack didn't move anything but his mouth. "Leave this place—or die," he rumbled. "You will not kill me. The spirits protect me. Your arm will wither, your gun melt in your hand. I curse you. You are cursed."

The Smith & Wesson was a double-action, and Basso didn't have to set back the hammer before he fired. The way the hammer clicked back sounded more important, I guess. "One last chance to go back to your chicken plucking," Basso said.

"Shoot," Doctor Jack sneered, raising his bloodstained hands. "No bullet can reach me."

Doctor Jack spoke to his congregation in some kind of lingo. They didn't move. I guess he was telling them to watch hard while he turned Basso's .45 into candlewax.

The heavy gun jerked in Basso's hand and Doctor Jack lost the middle finger on his right hand. A doctor couldn't have done a neater job. The bullet took the finger off right at the knuckle. Doctor Jack didn't look any more surprised than Basso would have been if the Smith & Wesson had turned to wax. No pain showed in the old black's face, just bewilderment. Kids look like that the first time they hear Santa Claus is a lie. I almost felt sorry for the old rat. It's a hell of a note to have your magic powers fail when you need them most.

I don't know why those thirty other blacks

didn't come at us, razors open and slashing. Doctor Jack looked at his hand as if he'd never seen it before. The other blacks looked at him, too surprised to decide which way to jump.

Basso bored in. The hammer of the .45 clicked back again. It was loud enough to get Doctor Jack's attention away from his missing finger. A flicker of fear showed in his eyes for a second, then it was gone.

"That first one was just a test," Basso said. The muzzle of the .45 moved around and Doctor Jack's eyes followed it, like one snake looking at another. The gun stopped moving. Basso said, "This one is the real thing."

I didn't know what Basso was going to do—I guess kill the old boy—and see what happened. The way I figured it, the congregation wanted Basso to shoot. Every congregation has its disbelievers and doubting Thomases—and this was one way to find out for sure.

Doctor Jack spoke up, and I was glad he did. I wanted the reverend to live to drink all the chicken blood his black heart desired: That way I had a good chance to stay alive. People who know about such things tell me being slashed with a razor doesn't hurt much. You just bleed to death and hardly know you're doing it. It was one of those stories I didn't want to test myself.

Doctor Jack was losing his hold on his flock, not because of anything that was said: you could feel it. The old boy said "Wait" to Basso; to his followers he said "You saw, my brothers. You saw the pistol aim for my heart and did not kill me. The spirits of the dead save Doctor

Jack. They take a finger to let Doctor Jack know they can protect him or let him die. It is a sign, my brothers. See! I do not look for the lost finger. It will grow back. The spirits has spoken . . ."

Basso's gun was still aimed at Doctor Jack's head. Holding a .45 out at the end of his arm can tire a man out. "Can it, Doc," Basso said.

Have you ever seen a black snake smile? For me, this was the first time. He smiled right after somebody outside rapped three long and three short raps on the street door. "No woman, no money," Doctor Jack said. "Never was here and now they gone. Sorry, captain. Look upstairs all you want."

For a second, I thought Basso was going to gut-shoot the old man. I swear I could hear the spring tensing in the Smith & Wesson as his thick finger began to squeeze. "Upstairs quick," he yelled at me. Doctor Jack didn't expect him to move so fast after the long palaver. The old bastard was trying to say something. The short-barreled .45 smashed him above the left eye, breaking the bone there, chopping through the eyebrow. Basso backhanded the .45 as he crashed past the old man and solid metal clunked against skullbone. Doctor Jack screamed, and the blows forced him down on his knees. The screaming woke up a crate of fat white chickens I hadn't noticed before.

"Cover them," Basso roared, running toward a rickety stairs in the back of the room. I don't know what he meant by cover them. How in hell do you cover twenty-five or thirty Voodoo blacks or any kind of blacks or whites—or any kind of people? I still couldn't figure why I was still alive, the way things were; I didn't give a good goddamn what happened to Basso. Both of us would have been dead and sliced to sandwich meat if the awful sight of Doctor Jack, battered and bloody, hadn't kept the other blacks bug-eyed and not knowing what to do next. They would make up their lie-rattled minds when they got around to it. I thought it would be nice if Detective Basso got back downstairs before the verdict on us was in.

I thought the rattletrap stairs would give under Basso's weight. But no good looking at him: I held the .45 steady on Doctor Jack, moving it a bit to include his more enthusiastic supporters.

The door at the head of the stairs was locked from the inside. It was as solid as the street door and Lord knows what went on up there when it was business as usual. I didn't think even a mad bull like Basso could knock it down. The way he went at it, I began to think the eleven thousand meant more to him than it did to me.

The big .45 blasted three times, and the door didn't give. I didn't see—I heard Basso step back and mulekick the door. Even so, it took four or five kicks before the wood tore loose from the lock.

Basso let loose two more shots before he shouldered the door off the hinges. Now Basso's gun was empty and that wasn't smart, but Basso was mad. He went in anyway with the empty .45

and I could hear furniture breaking and Basso cursing.

Doctor Jack tried to get up off his knees. I told him to stay there. A window broke upstairs, and I knew Basso was good and mad. On his knees, the blood blinding his right eye, Doctor Jack was glaring at me with the other eye. I guess he hadn't paid much heed to me while Basso was threatening his life. I didn't like the way he looked at me. Maybe he had figured out who I was. The hard hat didn't go with my sun-baked face; I don't know what it was.

Basso came clumping down the stairs in his man-kicking shoes. The .45 was in his hand, and he was pushing fresh shells into the chamber. The stairs creaked under his weight. "Gone— the whore is gone out the back window," he said, more to himself than to me. "I smelled her back at the hotel, I smell her now. But she's gone out the window."

That explained the rapping on the door. I had a feeling the yellow man Xavier was in it.

My thought was to get the hell out of there, to follow the girl, naturally—but mostly to get my carcass out of there. Basso, by God, was pressing his luck. He came over and yanked Doctor Jack to his feet and slapped him. When his hand stopped slapping the palm was smeared with blood.

I wanted to get out of there. Later he could come back and strangle Doctor Jack with his own yellow guts, and it was all right by me. What I didn't want was to let the girl get away with my eleven thousand while Basso wore out his crazy temper.

"Let's go, Basso," I said. "Maybe we can still catch her."

Basso jerked the gun halfway up toward me. God, but he was boiling over! "Go on—chase the whore! Run out, you god-blasted cowboy! But this stinking nigger is going to hang." Basso slapped Doctor Jack again, pointed his .45 at the old boy's followers. I didn't know a middling-old man like Basso could get so mad. "Come on, you chicken-sucking savages."

There wasn't a sound. Basso was all surprise. It was like the time long ago when Daniel Boone gobbled like a wild turkey at those Indians, and it surprised them so much they ran away. Of course, that was more than a hundred years before and the here and now was New Orleans, 1891, and these were blacks, not Indians.

Basso was making a mistake taking Doctor Jack out of there. But I thought I had to back him up. I don't know why I thought that. To me, sure as shooting, it was a waste of time.

"You go first," I said.

Chapter Ten

Doctor Jack's deep voice rose to a wild scream as Basso dragged him out of there. The lingo he was spouting was French and Spanish seasoned well with Voodoo talk. You didn't have to understand it to know he was calling on the spirits to strike us dead. Getting no help from the other world, he told his bully boys to do the job with their razors.

They started to move toward us, still shocked out of their skulls by Jack's downfall, but taking orders is a hard habit to break. They didn't exactly move; they flowed across the room like a mudslide. That was how I felt—a man trying to shoot a mudslide with a revolver.

Basso put the muzzle of the Smith & Wesson under Doctor Jack's right ear. The hammer was back, and his finger was closed on the trigger. Nothing quiets a man like the cold mouth of a .45 pistol. Doctor Jack's mouth was open, but nothing came out it. "Tell them to hold up,"

Basso told him. "One more move and you lose your shiny head."

Doctor Jack spoke again in Voodoo language, and they stopped coming—all but two big blacks. The old boy didn't like that; he yelled at them. Razors slipped from their sleeves into their hands and flipped open. "Go back," Doctor Jack yelled in English.

Basso and Doctor Jack were behind me; the two blacks slashed at me first. The one closest had long arms and nearly got me in the neck. Thin steel sliced through the collar of my coat, and if it cut the flesh I didn't feel it. I shot the first black in the chest, the other in the head, and I had to put another bullet in the first man before he fell down.

Smoke curled from the muzzle of the gun— the only thing that moved in the room. As they say, it was now or never. Two down—twenty-eight to go! I eased around to one side of the squat doorkeeper. Something warm trickled down my chest under the shirt, and I knew what they said about razors was true. A few inches higher and it would have been the jugular.

"Open it," I told the doorkeeper. I didn't put the gun in his back; once you touch a man with a gun he knows where to grab. Doctor Jack yelled at him, and he threw the bolts. The door swung open, and I cracked him across the back of the neck. The way he staggered was like a drunk trying to decide where to fall down. I helped him find a place.

Basso walked Doctor Jack out first, and I knew there were men waiting in the dark, but nothing happened right away. Basso knew it, too, and he yelled, "Listen good, you sons of bitches. I got your witch doctor, and I'll kill him quick, the first one tries anything."

Doctor Jack hollered long and loud in that secret lingo. I hoped he was agreeing with Basso. I went out the door backwards, with three bullets left in my gun and not completely sure I would ever see Texas again.

The few lights that showed when we went in had gone out, and the narrow street was dark as a coffin with the lid screwed down. There was no noise, none at all; Darktown was holding its breath. A thin shaft of light slanted from the door of Doctor Jack's church, then that, too, went out. The light went out, but the door didn't close.

I followed Basso down the middle of the cobblestoned street. It was just barely possible to make him out in the reflected glare of the city lights. Basso's heavy boots moved quickly and quietly over the cobblestones, and Doctor Jack didn't make any noise at all.

I found myself counting, and a long minute took us to the corner. They started shooting at us when we came around it. Five or six guns spat flame from street level, and then a rifle opened up from a second floor window. A knife came at me from behind; I didn't hear it until it cut through the air beside my head. A black shape jumped at me, and I shot it in midair. Another shape jumped after it and got its hands around my neck. I slammed the gun against the side of the attacker's head, and the hands held on until the skullbone cracked.

Doctor Jack was screaming like a madman, trying to break Basso's armhold. Basso held Jack and fired back at the gun flashes. Bullets whanged off the cobblestones, zipping like hornets. I heard the yellow man shouting orders. Basso wasn't getting anywhere with Doctor Jack, and when I heard a muffled shot I knew Basso had killed the old man with a bullet in the back of the neck.

The body hit the street, and I fell over it. The rifleman in the window put a bullet where I would have been standing if I hadn't tripped. Basso was crouched down by the side of a house, shooting back while bullets broke plaster above his head. The rifleman stopped to reload, and I fired at the next flash and got him.

I wasn't sure until the body fell into the street. "Jesus!" Basso cursed. "I'm hit in the chest."

My gun was empty. I tried to take his. "Shells in my pocket," he said. "Load my gun, too. I can't move my goddamn arm."

I thumbed shells into Basso's gun and put it in his left hand. A bullet scattered plaster dust in my face. Basso fired, and a man screamed. I had to fire three times before I killed another one. "Can you move?" I asked Basso.

"Better than you," he roared. "Let's go."

Just then a match flared, and a bunch of oil-soaked rags sailed through the darkness. I killed the man who threw the light, and we came around the corner shotting at everything that moved. Another bullet buried itself in Basso's chest, but he kept going. "Leave me be," he roared when I tried to help him.

Our guns knocked down three more blacks, and I dropped another shooter who opened up from inside a window. Xavier, the yellow man, fired fast with a handgun before he ducked into an alley. There was another alley across the street, and they fired at us from both sides. Staggering and roaring, Basso took one side; I took the other.

Then we were through the crossfire, and they were out in the street again, coming after us, firing as they came. The skin on the point of my elbow was touched by a bullet. We reloaded on the run. I did the reloading, passing the gun back to Basso. Every time we stopped to shoot it was harder for Basso to go on. I don't know how many blacks we dropped—a lot—but they kept coming. When one black was killed another picked up his gun and kept coming.

Basso started to fall. I grabbed him and he cursed me. "Save your strength, you dumb bastard," I roared back at him. Some men pray when they're going to die; Basso favored cursing. I caught him under the good arm and started to drag. It was like dragging a locomotive.

"No use," Basso groaned. "There's no feeling in my legs. Get the hell away from here."

"Not yet," I said. My gun had a full chamber and I emptied as fast as I could pull the trigger. An unhitched wagon stood outside a stableyard. It was rotten cover, but it was all we had. I shoved Basso under the wagon and rolled in after him. After I reloaded Basso's gun, I tried to keep it.

They couldn't see us now, and they spaced out, coming slow. On my belly, I did better shooting. Two of them fell down before a hail of lead started taking the wagon body apart. All the blood in Basso's body was coming out through the holes in his chest. No matter what happened, he didn't have long. "Put the hat under my arm, then do what I say. Run, you shit-kicker. When you catch the whore, give her one for me."

"That's a promise," I said. There weren't enough bullets to load both .45's. Basso got a full load; I got three. I started to crawl out from behind the wagon. With the wagon between me and the blacks I might have a chance. "Be seeing you, Basso," I said. "We all get it some time."

Air wheezed in and out of Basso's chest wounds: The son of a bitch was trying to laugh. "You're a lucky fella, cowboy. The minute we got the money I'd have killed you."

"Maybe," I said. The firing was heavy again, and Basso fired back as I started to run. I got fifty feet before they spotted me, but Basso held them. He held them, his arm propped up by that fool hat, firing until the chamber was empty. Then they were all over him, shooting and stabbing.

The ones who hadn't stopped to chop up Basso were still coming after me. I hoped to hell I was running the right way. That way was where Rampart Street was supposed to be. A man running in boots is no match for bare feet. Behind me I could hear bare feet slapping over cobblestones, and the sound kept getting closer. There was some light in the next street, and when I turned I could see the yellow man out in front of the others.

There was no way to outrun him. I steadied the short-barreled .45 and fired. The bullet didn't hit him. He was a lot closer when I fired again. He was so close I could see the machete in one hand, the handgun in the other. The bullet hit him in the middle of the belly, and he kept running until his brain told his body it was time to die.

Police whistles started to blow; a bell joined in. Isn't it something? I could have bear-hugged those dirty grafting New Orleans bulls. When I looked back the only man in the street was the fella I'd just killed. The murdering bastards just faded away into the darkness. And so did I.

I ducked into an alley and watched a patrol wagon full of uniformed bulls rattle past. The man sitting beside the driver rang the bell, and I knew there was going to be some fun when they found Basso's body. After some more dodging, I made my way back to Rampart Street.

Even in a wild town like New Orleans, a man with shirt and coat soaked with blood gets noticed. I hoped most of the blood was Basso's. I was tired but not weak, and the slice from the razor didn't hurt much. Tell the truth, I didn't exactly know what to do next. Well, yes, I meant to get myself a new suit of clothes; beyond that I'd have to sit down with a bottle and think a spell before coming to any important decisions.

I sort of missed Basso. Of course, I wasn't sorry the big bull was dead. Still, he did know the dirty old town like the back of his hairy paw, and I didn't know it at all. What I did know I didn't like. I didn't know where to find a clothing store, for instance. I walked along Rampart Street feeling like a fool. A uniformed policeman big as a buffalo was parading along the other side of the street. If he got friendly, I thought I'd tell him I fell down in a slaughterhouse. That was a damn fool idea, and I knew it. I knew I'd have to kill him with the last bullet in my gun.

But he passed like a riverboat on a picnic cruise. Finally, I picked out the worst looking citizen I could find, and asked him for directions. He was the first cockeyed man I ever saw with only one eye. It made him sour on his fellow man, I guess, and I had to slap him in the jaw to make his mouth move. "Benjamin's Dry Goods around the corner on Gravier Street.

I turned him loose, and he scurried off like a sick coyote. When he got far enough away, he yelled something dirty after me. Lord, I thought, what a town!

Benjamin was a man of the world or else his eyesight wasn't so good. The blood didn't bother him a bit. Sure he could sell me a suit, the latest model. He tried to sell me two suits when I peeled off some of Hindman's money. In the end, I settled for a black worsted suit, two shirts, a tie, and a wide-brimmed fedora hat.

I kept an eye on the old geezer while I changed my duds behind a curtain. The razor slash wasn't nothing to fret about. I guess the suit-seller wasn't interested in how I got so bloody. He went back to counting a stack of pants, and the only time he looked up was when I tore one of the shirts to make a bandage.

I got out of there fast, with the old storekeeper telling me how well I looked, and ran after a trolley and climbed aboard. Three blocks from there I jumped down and went into a saloon. I stood at the bar and put away four drinks and thought about Minnie Haha.

Sure, I decided—why not? I had chased this murdering female all over New Orleans. Every place she lit down somebody died. One way or another, she was a champion at killing or causing people to be killed—Gertie, Nails, Hindman's two boys, her brother. After Doctor Jack I stopped counting. Like Basso said, I was no detective. Minnie could have run out of places to hide, or there could be no end of places. Now it wasn't going to be so easy for her to hide, not in New Orleans, not when Basso's man Frank connected her with the Chief's death. All they had to do was dig up the Blue Book and they'd know what she looked like. They had no hard evidence on Minnie, but people have a way of talking after they've been in the back room for a while.

My guess was that Minnie would keep running. But where? God damn it! It was more than an hour since Basso went up those stairs and found her gone. It would be another hour, maybe two, before they had a description and started watching the railroad stations and the riverboats. By then, she could be on a train for points north or west. Maybe on a boat for Tampico. Or—my guess—on her way to St. Phail.

That's what it was—a hunch, a feeling in my gut. Home is where most people run when they use up the other places. St. Phail was one of the places the law would check. I figured to beat them to it. Then, if she wasn't there, the hell with it! I'd just have to live with the Gertie killing if, after going over all the facts, they decided to pin the tail on me. St. Phail would be my last stop in Louisiana; after that, good or bad, back to Texas.

The bartender said the South Rampart Street Station was what I wanted. Right down the street. I walked down there, and nobody tried to stop me. There was a gun shop across from the station. I bought a box of forty-fives, then bought a ticket to Leesville after looking at the big map on the station wall. Leesville was the closest I could get to Minnie's hometown by train.

There was a twenty minute wait, and I went into the station barbershop and told the man to give me the works—haircut, shave, hot towels. On the train I'd be a sitting duck if the police came through, and the barbershop looked like a pretty good place to stay out of the way. The barber was still fooling with my hair when the train-caller yelled the last all aboard. I threw money at the barber and ran.

The train started to move and, by God!, it was good to get out of New Orleans. I put my feet up and pulled the new hat down over my eyes. The conductor came through to punch the tickets, and told me to get my dirty boots off the seat. I did what I was told. Later a sandwich butcher came along, and I bought some bad-colored beef between two slices of stale bread. I hadn't put food in my belly for close to twenty-four hours; the sandwich tasted fine.

The thought came to me that Minnie might be on the same train. I was so damn sick of chasing Minnie, but I went through the train, one end to the other, and didn't find her. No, the conductor said when I caught up with him, there was nobody aboard wno answered to that description. Maybe she was on the express; the express had pulled out thirty minutes earlier.

I wen back tc my seat and grabbed some sleep.

Chapter Eleven

It was two o'clock in the morning when the local pulled into Leesville. It was a fair-sized town, and it had gone to bed. Scratching and yawning, the station agent told me to try Sanders Livery Stable for a horse. He told me how to get there.

It took some active door-rattling to get the stablekeeper out of bed. "Now why can't folks arrange to do business during daylight hours?" he complained, stuffing his nightshirt inside his pants. "This is the second time tonight I been woke. First by a woman and now you. Tell me something, mister, what's a woman want with a horse and buggy in the middle of the night?"

"Maybe she wants to go some place," I said.

He eyed me suspiciously when I described Minnie, said I was her cousin Haywood from Bogalusa. That we got separated in New Orleans, that I was worried sick about her traveling alone late at night.

"We got to charge extra renting horses at night," he said. He gave a creaky laugh. "Plus holding money should you injure the animal."

I gave him the money.

"I guess that's the female," he said. "Come in on the express. Said she had to get over to St. Phail in a hurry. I told her she'd be smart to wait till morning, but, no, it had to be on tonight." I climbed onto a brown gelding and rode out the west road. About ten miles out straight, no forks, the stableman advised me. There was good light, and I put some life into the animal with my boots. About an hour later a sign told me I was about to enter the village of St. Phail.

It wasn't much more than a wide place in the road—bigger than Hindman said, but not much. Mostly what it was—a post office, a few stores, a scatter of houses. There was no sign of any law office; the nearest law would be Leesville. I walked the horse through the town and out the other side. The crickets and bullfrogs were having a concert; they stopped and started again. A dog barked for a while, then lost interest. There still wasn't any sign of the Verrier place.

There was a crossroads with signs saying Slage and Hawthorn. I almost didn't see the rotting sign, the painted letters peeling off, that said Verrier House. The arrow was pointed at the the ground, but I got the idea. One mile, the sign stated.

I passed some Negro cabins by the side of the road. Trees grew in close to the road, and it was dark for a couple of hundred yards. Out of the trees, I saw the bulk of the big house, a single light coming from a downstairs window. In a way, this was where it all started; I hoped to finish it in the same place.

Two stone pillars had given up trying to support the heavy iron gates. The sagging gates had been open for a long time, and weeds and briars were tangled in the bars. A curved carriageway lined with poplars ran up to the house from the road; weeds and grass grew up through the gravel. The gelding's hooves made hardly a sound as I led him toward the house.

In the moonlight, the house still looked like what it had been. When I got closer, I saw some of the windows were broken and part of the roof had fallen in. Halfway up the drive I walked the gelding across the ruined lawn and hitched him good to an apple tree. Then I went back to the drive and up to the house.

The horse and buggy stood at the foot of the crumbling steps; the front door was open. I went up the steps with the Smith & Wesson in my hand; beautiful Minnie was a killer, and I was through taking chances. Light came from a big room off the darkened main hallway. I was close to the arch that led into the lighted room when I heard a woman's voice. I stopped and listened. She was still where I couldn't see her, but the talking went on. I waited for someone to answer, and nobody did. Nothing that was being said made any sense to me; it was English, but the words ran together. Then she started to laugh.

"Don't move, Minnie," I said coming into the light, the .45 cocked and ready. "I'll kill you."

Minnie lay on a big sofa heaped with dirty pillows, waving her arms and laughing. I told her again, and she stopped laughing. The gun in my hand didn't scare her; it started her laughing again. She clapped her hands together like a child, then held them against the sides of her face, again like a child expecting a treat.

"Put them behind your head," I said. "Then stand up and keep them there."

Her eyes were crazy, and the laughing didn't stop. But she got up, and I went over to her. "A gentleman come to call," she said. "And we haven't even been properly introduced."

"Stand still," I warned her.

"Still as a statue. Quiet as a churchmouse. Soft as a summer breeze," my friend Minnie said. "Hey, what's your name?"

Minnie was crazy or doing a good job of pretending. I didn't search her: I ripped the low-necked green dress from breasts to crotch. No guns, no knives fell out of it, and there was no place to hide anything else: All she wore was the dress.

The torn dress fell around her ankles. She giggled. "That wasn't gallant, sir," she said, stepping out of it.

I was tired of her act. A stiff-handed slap jerked her head to one side; no pain showed in the crazy eyes. "The hand is quicker than the thigh," she said. "Listen, honestly, you want to know why Jefferson Davis wore red suspenders? You give up? I'll tell you—to keep his shoulders down."

"Where's the eleven thousand dollars?"

"Oh, that. Why it's over there in that leather

bag. You want some? Hey, are you a robber? No, you don't look like a robber. Don't tell me— you're taking up a collection for the new school-house."

I looked in the leather bag and found the money. It looked like some of it was gone. "Look under the money, and you'll find some white envelopes," Minnie said. "Pass one of them over, there's a nice man. A girl has to take her medicine."

I guess I was dumb. "Medicine?" I said.

Minnie wasn't laughing now and her eyes were getting dull. I think she was beginning to remember who I was. "Medicine for me," she said. "Cocaine. Lovely white powder."

I should have figured something like that but, well, I was just an old country bank robber. Basso hadn't figured it either, or if he did he didn't tell me. The kind of people I knew used whiskey to go crazy; cocaine was something I didn't know about, didn't think about. I knew there were people used it in the cities, that once you started snuffing it up your nose you couldn't stop, that it drove you crazy if you took enough of it.

"Give it here, you son of a bitch," Minnie screamed. She started at me with her claws raised. The gun didn't stop her, and I had to use my fist. The punch knocked her back on the sofa, and she sprawled there, screaming and shaking, begging for it.

That was the big trouble with nose candy, as the clickers called it. The effects wore off after a very short time. Minnie had been snuffing before

I got to the house; that explained the talking and laughing.

"Please," she said. She knew me now. "Please, Carmody. Let me have some, then you can kill me."

"No deal," I said. "First you talk. Then you write out a confession and sign. How you killed Gertie, and why—everything. Somehow or other, you started taking this stuff. But there was no money here, so you went to New Orleans. Nothing you could work at, supposing you wanted to work, would bring in enough money to buy your poison. So you became a house girl at Gertie's. You were drugged all the time, so Gertie decided to make a freak out of you. After that you were Minnie Haha, the cold fish that couldn't be caught, but you didn't give a damn as long as there was money for snuff. Gertie kept you supplied, but maybe she held out sometimes to keep you in line. Nails came from St. Phail, and you could have known him."

Minnie's eyes were dull, so was her voice. "I knew him," she said. "We had the same mother."

I showed her one of the little white envelopes. "What about your father?" The thing about being Nails' half-sister took me by surprise. It explained the dark skin.

Minnie showed her hate. "My father was a doctor. The Nails family cropped for us. He raised me and my brother as white, but I never believed his story that he had been married to a Creole girl from New Orleans. I didn't find out for sure until a couple of years ago. That's when

136

I started using cocaine. My father was dead, but there was a lot of it left in his office. I used it to forget I was a nigger. Later I didn't give a damn . . ."

"Not yet," I said. I wanted to get it all straight. "Nails tried to protect you—hated Gertie for a lot of reasons. But mostly because of you. Half-sister or not, you were sleeping with Nails. The only place you could go was the Hotel La Hache. Maybe Gertie got wind of it—I don't know. Anyway, when the chance to kill Gertie, blame somebody else, and steal eleven thousand dollars came along, you grabbed it. Only Nails got killed and I didn't run."

"I could buy all the cocaine in the world with eleven thousand dollars," Minnie said dully. "It would be there whenever I wanted it. Nobody telling me what to do. How much I could take. I didn't care what I had to do to get it."

The room was warm, but Minnie shivered. She looked at the envelope in my hand while she talked. "Please," she whispered.

"Be a brave girl," I said, remembering all that had happened. It was all coming together at last. "You did the planning, Nails the killing. You panicked and ran when you saw me, saw Nails was dead. You ran to the La Hache. You couldn't take your medicine in the street. Your brother, desperate for money, tracked you there. Or maybe he knew. He tried to grab some of the money, and you stabbed him. I know everything else. Where's the knife, Minnie?"

"I threw it away," she said. "I didn't want to kill George." Her voice rose to a scream. "But,

Jesus, he tried to take my money. You understand—I didn't want to kill anybody. I just
wanted the money."

"A clear case of self defense," I told her sour-
ly. "Now, Minnie, you're going to write it all
down. After that you get the cocaine."

"I won't do it," she said.

"I'll make a fire of it," I said. Keeping the gun
on her, I looked in the drawer of a broken writ-
ing desk and found some yellowed notepaper.
The inkwell was dry, but I found a pencil. I took
the pencil and paper over to Minnie, and said,
"Write what I tell you."

"What'll happen to me?" she wanted to know.

I stuck the pencil in her hand. "We'll get to
that later," I said. "You want the snuff, or not?"

"I'd like to kill you," she screamed. A slap
stopped the screaming, but the shaking went on.

"Address it to the Chief of Police, New Orleans," I said . . .

Minnie began to write. The pencil scratched
across the paper, and I made her begin at the
beginning and go on from there. The way her
hand shook, it took some time before it was finished.

"Sign it," I said.

She signed it, and held out her hand for the
envelope. When the envelope was torn open she
creased it, held back her head, and snuffed the
powder up her nose. That was how they did it
all right. Having her drugged might make it
easier to rope her to a chair, lay the confession
beside her, then ride off and send word to the
Leesvill sheriff from the first town I came to.

This was one time I was ready to give the law a helping hand.

The cocaine acted right away. It must be powerful stuff, the way it calmed Minnie, put the shine back in her eyes. Lying back on the sofa, bare and brown, she whispered more to herself than to me—"So peaceful."

Peaceful was how I wanted her. "That's fine," I said. "Just stand up and you'll be fine." It looked like George Verrier had fed and slept in the same room. All kinds of junk piled up beside the fireplace; there was a coiled rope lying on top of a worn saddle. I got the rope, and when I came back with it Minnie hadn't moved.

"Up," I said, starting to lift her into a straightbacked chair. One of her hands was buried in the cushions and came up holding a knife. In a second she turned into a screaming stabbing maniac. The double-edged knife laid open my face before I grabbed her wrist, but the drug made her strong as a man, and I couldn't make her let it go. Kicking and screaming, she sank her teeth into my wrist and the knife stabbed at my heart. I grabbed it again and turned it, and still Minnie wouldn't let go.

Now the knife was between us, the point inches from her chest. I didn't want to kill her, but suddenly the fight went out of her and she jerked the knife forward. The thin blade went into her, and her lips opened wide and then started to glaze. I didn't try to pull out the knife. It wouldn't have done any good. Minnie— Miss Frances Verrier—was beyond cocaine, beyond the hangman, beyond everything.

I made a neat job of it before I left. After I stretched her out on the couch, I put her hand around the shaft of the knife, the confession on a chair beside her. The cocaine was explained in the confession, and I left it in the leather bag where the law would find it later.

I didn't bother to count my money before I went outside and stowed it in the saddlebag. All in all, it had been one hell of a visit to New Orleans. Come morning, maybe before, the law would be on its way; it was time to get out of there. I had set out to prove I didn't kill Gertie, to get back my eleven thousand, and now I wanted to get as far away as that stolen horse would take me.

The Texas line was some place west of where I was—and I headed that way.

THE KILLERS

THEY ALL WENT FOR
THEIR GUNS AT ONCE . . . .

Kessler was faster than the others, but they were all good
boys. None of them got off a shot, though, or if they did
I didn't hear it. The 8-gauger boomed once in my hands and
the three riders turned into meat. Kessler was closer than
the others and he took the main charge. There was plenty
of lead left over for the other. It didn't just knock them off
their feet while it killed them. It sent them rolling and kept
them rolling. . . .

CHAPTER ONE

My cousin Luke is the kind of sheriff there ought to be more of. It wouldn't help to make folks any more honest, but there would be a better feeling all 'round. Luke had been sheriff of Brewster County in South Texas for close to ten years when this business with Big Sam Thornton got started. Of course, I didn't know that or I'd have stayed away from Salter City, where Luke was headquartered. Not that old Luke would have turned me out, but, after all, do you know any sheriffs would have jumped to claim a fella like me as a cousin?

The fact was, I didn't know where Luke was or

what he was doing. I thought about Luke about once every two years, and that's how worried I was about his welfare. I got shot during some trouble up in New Mexico, and one of the holes in me was still giving me trouble. The law was interested in me for a few things, and I figured to take what money I had left and ride down into Old Mexico and drink tequila in the sun until I felt better and was ready to plan new business.

Salter City, in Brewster County, was on the way. Down that way it's hot and dry and wilder than the Dakota Badlands, country fit only for Gila monsters and Texans. I was being nice to myself, lying late in my blankets, traveling by day till I got sick of it, then bedding down early. When I got to Salter City I stopped for a drink and a meal cooked by somebody else.

It was about noontime, the town baking in the sun, and I was in some saloon drinking a warm, flat beer when Luke came in. I saw the badge before I saw who was wearing it. When you're on the dodge, which is what I seem to be most of the time, you get that way. Sometimes the lawmen in the real quiet towns are the worst, because they have nothing better to do than walk heavy around strangers passing through. I got set for the same old questions and answers. "New in town, ain't you"—all that hosspiss.

There was none of that. This sheriff was grinning all over his leathery face. "What took you so long, Carmody?" the sheriff asked.

"Hello, Luke," I said, surprised and glad to see

him—and not so glad. We'd done some wild things together as kids, but that was a long time ago— close to twenty years—and now Luke was a sheriff and I was dodging down to Mexico.

Luke came up close, grinning like mad. "That all you got to say, cousin? All these years and you say hello. You won't believe this, but you're the man I just been thinking about."

"What were you thinking?" I asked, still tensed up a bit.

Luke laughed and told the bartender to put another glass on the bar. "What in hell are you standing up for, Carmody? Come on over here and sit down."

Luke carried the bottle and the glasses. Looking at him, I couldn't see that twenty years had done much to Luke. Leathery sure, but then Luke had always been leathery; of no special age. I guess he sort of looked like me; about three years older was all. One thing he still was, and that was lazy. Even as a boy, Luke would never stand up when he could sit down, and never sit when he could lie. A big eater, too, and now it showed.

"We'll drink your bottle first," he said, "but you won't pay for it. I won't pay for it either. Folks around here just hate to take my money. A sheriff's money is no good, they tell me. How the hell are you, Carmody?"

I don't remember what I told him.

Luke grinned at me and knocked back two quick drinks. "Nobody asked you what you been doing, cousin. I said how you feel?"

"Good, Luke," I said. "On my way to Old Mexico."

Luke poured a drink for me. "There you go again, cousin. Telling me what you been doing and what you plan to do. A word—I know what you been doing."

"Not in Brewster County," I said. "I guess that's what you are—sheriff of Brewster County."

"You guess fine, Carmody. It ain't much, but it's all I got. Another word—I got it good."

The son of a bitch hadn't changed one bit. Back home, Luke used to worry his folks sick with all his schemes to get rich the easy way. First, after reading about Cyrus McCormick and Sam Morse, it was inventions all the time. One of Luke's earliest inventions was a real pip. Naturally, we all thought he was crazy. This invention was for city men, and the way Luke saw it, it would be a godsend and an act of mercy. You know what it was? It was a thing where a city man could tip his hat to a lady without taking his hands out of his pockets. It worked by squeezing a rubber ball with a rubber tube running under the clothes from pocket to hat. The squeezed air caused some damn thing under the hat to rise. Luke was good and mad when he wrote to the Patent Office in Washington and was told that some other fool had invented the same thing. . . .

I mentioned the hat-tipper to Luke.

"Never did catch on, did it?" he said.

"Some day they'll see how wrong they were," I said.

Luke took off his hat and set it on the table. For a man who said he was doing so good, Luke was dressed more like a drunken dentist with dirty tools than a moneyed sheriff. He wore one of those white shirts that are supposed to go with a collar, except that Luke didn't have a collar and the shirt wasn't anything like the driven snow the lady poets like so much.

"Being county sheriff is the best invention of all," Luke said. "Works as smooth as a Massachusetts watch if you keep it oiled right. Of course, there are folks keep trying to feed sand into the works. That's why I was thinking on you a while back. This very morning, in fact."

"You told me that, Luke."

Luke was still grinning, but his eyes were careful. "You ain't tried to kill President Garfield? You never spit on the flag? Don't suppose you never killed a man didn't need killing in some way?"

"I suppose," I told him, not getting his point, whatever it was. There was no telling with Luke.

"Glad to hear it, cousin," he said. "How'd you like to be acting sheriff of Brewster County for a spell? Maybe three weeks."

I pointed to the half empty bottle and Luke laughed. After that, he poured two more drinks and looked at the single bartender who was looking at us. "Fetch another bottle, Charley, then go out back and feed the chickens or something," Luke suggested.

"Thanks for reminding me, Luke," the barkeep said.

"You're not drunk and maybe you're not crazy," I said. "Then what?"

"Careful," Luke said, "is what I am. You want the job or not?"

I said no.

Luke put a doleful look on his seamed face. "Twenty-odd years a man don't see his cousin, then he asks one small favor, and gets told no. That ain't right, cousin. Since the family spirit seems dried up in you, does four hundred—say five hundred—change your mind?"

I was low on folding money. "Say it straight, cousin," I said.

"You married, Carmody?"

I guess Luke knew the answer to that, because he didn't wait for an answer. "Me neither," he said. "But I'm fixing to be. Been corresponding with the daintiest little thing through one of those matrimonial agencies in Baltimore, Maryland. Exchanged pictures and everything. This little gal allows that I'm sort of handsome in a craggy kind of a way . . ."

Luke looked at me like a country shit-kicker, and who was I to call the lady a liar?

"In a nut, I proposed and was accepted," Luke said. "Lorena, that's her name, says she's ready to come out West by herself, but I won't have it. This is no country for a woman, a pretty woman, on her lonesome. I told her that more than a month ago and now I'm afraid she's getting kind of jittery. That's why I got to go East and fetch her."

"What's stopping you?"

"Nobody here I can rightly trust with the job," Luke explained. A popular man I am with some folks—not with everybody. A man leaves the store untended or in the wrong hands, there's no telling what might happen. Sure would like to get married. Much as I'd like that, I'd hate to lose what I got here. Cousin, I'm too old to work."

"You always were," I said. That five hundred looked good to me, but Luke was still my cousin; and some things count.

"I got posters on me," I said. "You know that."

"I don't know what you got on you. You got nothing on you here."

"Not in Brewster County."

"I don't see beyond that. Beyond that I got bad eyesight and poor hearing. Will you do it, cousin? I got nobody else. Three weeks. Not more than that."

"Sure," I said. "How soon you plan to leave?"

"Soon's I can saddle my horse," Luke answered cheery as blazes. He fished an extra star out of his vest pocket and leaned over to pin it to my shirt. "No need to get up, cousin, just raise your right hand and repeat after me ..."

That was how I got to be acting sheriff of Brewster County, Texas. Luke said there was nothing to it. "We got some pretty wild boys in these parts, but mostly they're good boys. Saturday is the most trouble. Keep the peace, don't let them burn the town, and don't shoot anybody 'less you have to. Then shoot low. Now I got to announce the new appointment."

13

I followed Luke outside into the sun, feeling just a mite foolish. Luke was a simple fella in some things. His way of making an announcement was to pull his gun and let off a couple of shots in the air. That brought them to the doors and windows.

"That gent with the sour face is Mayor Dunstan," Luke whispered to me. "We don't exactly get along, but there's not a thing he can do about it."

Jerking his thumb in my direction, Luke yelled out the good news, and I must say the town folk didn't start any wild cheering. Maybe I looked too much like Luke. "Carmody'll take good care of the town," Luke roared. "A more dedicated acting sheriff there never was."

Now that it was done, all Luke could think about was getting to Baltimore. I managed to pry loose fifty dollars from him before he waved and started for the livery stable at a heavy trot.

"Ain't you going to pack?" I called after him.

In a minute, Luke was a cloud of dust heading north out of town. And there I was, standing in the middle of the main street with a sheriff's badge on my shirt.

I guess I'd been in Salter City all of twenty minutes.

CHAPTER TWO

I was sitting in a rocker in front of the sheriff's office when four men rode in behind a man in fancy clothes driving a buckboard. Luke had been gone two days, and when somebody said hello to me I said hello right back. That was about as deep into the job as I'd gone at the time.

The man in the buckboard touched his hat with his finger as he went by. I didn't remember who he was until he climbed down in front of the town's one hotel and gave the reins to one of the riders. Malachi Fallon was who he was, and suddenly I got the feeling that life in Salter City wasn't going

15

to be all that simple. Even without Fallon, the four hard cases would have been enough to tell me that.

Just about everybody in South Texas knew Malachi Fallon from his campaign posters. Some years back they were tacked up on every tree and barn door in that part of the state. He never did get to Washington or even to Austin, and after two windy campaigns he gave up. The last I'd heard of him he was running his own candidates up in Pecos County, trying to get at the pie in a roundabout way. Texans don't always show good sense, but they knew what they were doing when they voted down Malachi Fallon. Some men are unfortunate in the way they look, and Fallon was one of them. One look at him and you knew he was a crook, not an honest crook, which is what you have to be to succeed in politics; Fallon was a crooked crook, though that didn't keep him from being popular with some people.

I wasn't a bit happy to see him in Salter City. It was the kind of forgotten one-horse town that you didn't come to unless you had a damn good reason, or you just stumbled over it, like me. I knew he wasn't passing through because there was nothing but badlands between the town and the Mexican border. Suddenly I found myself grinning. Here I was starting to act like a real sheriff.

Whatever it was, Fallon's business must have been fairly important, because it wasn't ten minutes later when he came out, climbed into the buckboard and took the road south out of town with the four hard cases trailing behind.

"Did you see who that was?" the hotel clerk said when I went over there to pass the time of time. "Malachi Fallon himself. I voted for him both times he ran."

That told me something about the clerk. "Where did he go?" I asked.

The clerk was still rattled by his brush with the great man. "Well, I don't think that I should say. Mr. Fallon spoke to me in confidence . . ."

I did what Luke would have done. I wasn't mean about it. In fact, I was smiling when I reached across the desk and took a firm hold on the clerk's necktie. Using it to pull him forward, I whispered in his ear. "It's all right, you can tell me," I said. "Now where's Fallon gone?"

"The Eldredge place," he said. "Two or three families, all related, live out there. I warned Mr. Fallon about them. They're a bad bunch."

I let him go. "And what did Mr. Fallon say to that?"

"Nothing. He said nothing. And he didn't say what his business was."

The clerk smirked at me, the only way he could get revenge for his crumpled tie. "Maybe you'd better ask him yourself. That's not to say you'll get an answer."

I went to a three-stool eating place down the street. It was run by a gabby old geezer who looked like he never got out in the sun. While he was frying up some ham, I asked him what he knew about this Eldredge clan. That bothered him

17

because all he wanted to talk about was Malachi Fallon.

He turned the ham in the skillet and pointed a fork at me. "A bad bunch. Came out here from Georgia some years back, the whole bunch of them. Can't even say how many of them there is. Anyway —a lot. Sheriff's had trouble with them from time to time. Mostly they keep to themself. I guess the sheriff made kind of a deal. They don't bother the town, he don't bother them."

That sounded like Luke all right, but it didn't tell me a thing.

"Trash is what they are," the old man said. "What they do out there is anybody's guess."

I finished my breakfast and went back to the jail. When I got sick of sitting out front in the rocker, I went inside and looked to see what Luke had in the way of guns. The gun that interested me was what they call a goose-gun, a heavy monster, big-bored and with the barrel cut short, more like a carry-about cannon than a shotgun. It was clean as a whistle, but I worked on it anyway, to pass the time.

I chained the guns to the rack and took myself a walk. I could see that being a sheriff took a lot of practice at doing nothing in particular. Funny thing, just before Fallon and his hard cases rode in I'd just about made up my mind that Salter City was the deadest town in Texas. Now I wanted to keep it that way.

It must have been close to two hours later when I heard them coming back. I watched them

18

through the office window. Now there were three hard cases instead of four and Fallon had lost his fancy hat somewhere along the way. The horse moved while Fallon was getting down, and the big man from Pecos County hauled off and kicked the animal in the side. Then he stomped into the hotel with the three gunmen trailing him like watchdogs.

It still wasn't law business, so I moped about some more. I broke open a bottle and drank some whiskey, and thought about Fallon. I thought about going over to say howdy-do, then decided against it. Maybe Fallon would come to me.

I set the chair where I could watch the hotel through the window. They didn't come out. Two boys from the livery stable came to take away the buckboard and the horses. Nothing else happened for a couple of hours.

I heard some shouting down the street and went outside to see what it was. It was trouble, the start of all the trouble. A thickset man with a beard was driving a wagon with a saddled horse tied behind. I stepped into the street and waited for the wagon to pull up. I knew there was a dead man in the bed of the wagon before I looked inside.

The farmer didn't have much to say. "Got something for you, Deputy. Found him dragging from the stirrup. Dead before that, I reckon."

The dead man was one of Fallon's hard cases. The farmer was right. Being dragged by his horse wasn't what killed him. There was a hole in his forehead, and he was long dead by the time his animal spooked and ran.

"Never seen him before," the farmer said. "You know him?"

"Where did you find him? Was it by the Eldredge place?"

The farmer looked scared. "Nobody said that. It was out that way. Nobody said the Eldredges done it. Not me, you bet."

I dragged the dead man out by the heels and when he hit the street he rolled. The back of his head was all blown away. I dragged the body up on the porch and went back into the cells to get a blanket to keep the flies away till burying time. People crowded in asking questions, but all the excitement wasn't enough to bring Fallon and his boys out of the hotel. While I was tucking in the dead man, I took a quick look at the hotel, but they didn't even show their faces.

"This town got an undertaker?" I asked one of the boys from the livery stable.

"Got a carpenter, he'll do," the kid said. "I'll go find him."

Now it was my business, so I left the corpse where it was and walked over to the hotel. There was nobody in the lobby except the clerk, and he was still mad about his necktie. "Up in his room resting," the clerk said. "What's going on out there in the street?"

"You just lost a customer," I told him. I pried the room number out of him without having to get tough about it. I knocked and the door opened right away. The hard case had one hand on the doorknob, one hand on his gun.

20

"I want to see Fallon," I said.

The hard case didn't budge. I guess he thought he had to act mean in front of his boss, or maybe he needed the practice. "Who're you?" he asked.

I seem to run into boys like that all the time. "I'm a drummer in ladies' underpants," I told him, tapping the badge with my left hand. "Where's Fallon?"

"Let him in," Fallon said from the bed. I went in but Fallon didn't get up. The two other hard cases sat in chairs by the window and there were glasses and a whiskey bottle on the dresser. I walked to the window, and from there I could see the jail with the dead man out front under the blanket.

Fallon watched me from the bed. "Something I can do for you, Sheriff?"

"Looks like you're short a man," I told him.

Fallon looked at the three gunmen. "I can count, Sheriff," he said.

Fallon had loose liver-colored lips and the words didn't come out of his mouth—they straggled out, as if he had trouble keeping his mind on the proceedings. Everything he said sounded tired and kind of sneering. Even with a smile I could see why the voters had turned him down. In spite of his fancy clothes, there was something dirty about the son of a bitch.

"A farmer just brought in one of your boys," I said. "He's dead but I guess you know that. I thought maybe you could tell me how it happened? Did the Eldredge boys do it?"

"Never heard of them," Fallon drawled. "Any of you boys know that name?"

They shook their heads. "There, you see," Fallon said. "Must have been somebody else shot Mike."

"Don't take it so hard," I said.

"Watch your mouth, Deputy," one of the hard cases warned me. "That's Malachi Fallon you're talking to."

"Not deputy—I'm the Sheriff. You got that now, have you? I'd like for you to try hard."

I guess I didn't sound much like a public servant. Fallon didn't like it.

Still not getting up, he said, "What's biting on you? You got something against my boys? Against me? You barged in here asking questions and we gave you answers. You asked about these Eldredge people and we said no. All right, somebody shot poor Mike when he wandered off by himself. What do you want us to do—tear our clothes like Indian women? You're the law. Go catch the killer."

"You didn't say anything about looking for your hat."

Fallon swung his legs off the bed and sat up. He snapped his fingers and one of the hard cases handed him a cigar, then lit it for him. "Don't push it too hard, friend," he said to me. "Save the smart talk for the Saturday drunks. You know who I am, you ought to know better than to crowd me."

Fallon laughed. "Hey, you're not planning to arrest us, are you, Sheriff? Being a lawyer, I'd have

22

to submit, but my three law clerks wouldn't like it."

Fallon's three law clerks guffawed at the great man's joke.

"Been nice talking to you, Sheriff," Fallon said. "Come around any time you need legal advice."

Fallon lay down again and put his hands behind his head, the cigar tilted in his flabby mouth. Eyes closed as if he couldn't stand to see any more of the world's hardships, he drawled for his supper. "One of you boys—I don't say which one—do a tired, hungry man a favor. Go down and tell that fool clerk I want that food today."

The three gunmen thought that was funny too. They thought everything Fallon said was funny when he wasn't laying into them.

I went out.

CHAPTER THREE

The old man who ran the restaurant told me how to get out to the Eldredge place, and I found it about where he said it was, five miles from town in a dead-end canyon in a scatter of low hills that ran up into the mountains. A trail forked away from the main road and I followed it, remarking to myself that it was pretty poor country to raise anything but snakes. None of the land around Salter City was any too good; and it looked like the late-arriving Eldredges had settled on the worst of it.

I rested my animal and looked at a sign that warned me to keep out or get shot. Just about every word on that sign was spelled wrong, but the meaning was clear. Hopefully, I took the star off my shirt pocket and pinned it high on my vest. Maybe they wouldn't shoot me right away if they saw the star. The sun was well past the mid-point between east and west, but it was still hot as a bunkhouse stove in a Montana winter. I gave the animal water and drank some myself. Maybe I was making too much out of Fallon's being in Salter City; still I had the feeling that big trouble was getting set to explode.

There was another sign as threatening as the first, and when I rode past it without stopping to spell out the words, a rifle cracked and a bullet touched the crown of my hat without taking it off my head. I reined in and waited. There was no more shooting, and that could mean the shooter was thrifty with his ammunition or that he was using a muzzle-loading rifle.

That's what he was using all right, a long-barreled small-caliber squirrel gun, and when he had another shot ready, he poked the long barrel out from behind a pile of rocks tangled over with bushes, and yelled at me to turn my animal and ride back the other way. He didn't ask me who I was, what I wanted. "You git," was all he said.

I could make out the rifle barrel; that was all. He sounded young, and that could be worse than old. I don't know how I knew he was sighting in on that damn sheriff's star. What I did know for sure was that a bullet from that long rifle would shove the lawman's badge halfway through my chest.

26

When I didn't move, he yelled, "You git and git fast. This here is private property. We don't allow nobody in here."

I yelled back that he was shooting at the county sheriff.

Whoever he was, he was a good shot and a slow thinker. It took him a while. "You ain't the sheriff," he yelled. "Even if you was t'wouldn't make no difference. I said nobody comes in here."

"I'm coming in," I said. "Now you signal your daddy and tell him that. Do that or shoot me. Then they'll hang you, sonny."

The boy with the long gun came up slowly from behind the rocks. Fallon's glossy hat was too big for him, so big that it came down halfway over his ears. The hat sure as hell didn't go with the bleached-out overalls he was wearing. He looked like what he was, a half savage, ignorant, dirty mountain youngster; and I knew he could put a bullet through any part of me he wanted.

"Stay still," he said. Then he let out the most godawful howl I ever heard from any man, white or Indian. The first howl was drawn out; he added a couple of yips at the end. He grinned before he remembered to look mean again. I didn't do anything.

It didn't take them long to get there. They didn't all come from the same direction; they swarmed in from all sides: men and boys from the snot-nosed age to well past seventy. And there wasn't one of them that wasn't toting some kind of rifle. I swear a man could put together a gun museum with the weapons they were pointing at me. More than twenty rifles in all. The young ones carried the oldest weapons, and some of their guns were old enough to have gone south during the Mexican War. The guns were old, but I wouldn't have bet a nickel that they wouldn't still shoot straight and true.

But there were new guns too. One of the new rifles was in the hands of a shaggy-bearded old man in an honest-to-god wool hat, a real mountain headpiece. The old man didn't take his fierce eyes off me while he spoke to the boy. After the boy explained, the old man rapped him across the skull with the barrel of the 44-40 Winchester. I guessed that was for not following orders to the letter, meaning that he should have killed or crippled me first, then started his howling.

The old man told the boy to pick up his dropped squirrel gun; and I was reminded of how a she-cougar teaches her cubs how to fight by batting them around. After saying something I couldn't make out, the old man came closer. Close enough to talk without yelling.

"You want to come in, then come on," he growled at me, suspicious as only a mountain man can be with strangers. "First you let your guns slide. That means all your guns. We find a hide-away gun in your bag we'll kill you. May do that anyhow."

They started a rush when my guns hit the dirt; the old man roared at them to get back. "You take charge, Willy," he told the boy with Fallon's hat.

They had my guns and I figured it wouldn't get me killed if I moved my hands. I tapped the star on my chest. "This mean nothing to you?"

The old man's eyes were red-rimmed and angry. I don't know what he was so mad about. Maybe it was just his way. "Less than dog shit," he told me. "You move your hands again you'll lose a finger. Let the reins go. We'll lead you in."

That's what they did. The boy with Fallon's fancy hat took the reins and that's how I got to see the Eldredge place, with every male Eldredge pointing a rifle at me, not just ready to kill me, but wanting to kill me. It was like they had brought their Smoky Mountain ways down to south Texas; and I wasn't about to argue one little bit. Not then anyway.

The trail took a turn between some big rocks, and then I saw the sprawl of cabins along a creek shaded by cottonwoods. The cabins were built mountain style and there was that good old mountain stink that you never forget once you smell it. There was a still going full blast out in the open. The smell of mash was the best smell on the place. A lot of women and girls stood around looking as mean-tempered as hostile Comanche squaws. Maybe not as clean and pretty as Comanche squaws. There were the usual starved mongrel dogs scratching and biting in the dust. Looking at the Eldredge place, I sure hoped old Luke was enjoying his vacation.

"Get down," the old man ordered. "You want a drink of whiskey?"

I guess I must have looked surprised.

"Common manners," the old man said. He didn't smile when he added, "Could be your last."

The boy called Willy was the old man's favorite. He ran to fill a tin cup with whiskey and gave it to the old man. The old man gave it to me. I tasted it. No doubt about it—the genuine article, old No. 1 Pop-Skull, all of five minutes old.

I wasn't a friend, so the old man didn't join me. He rooted in his overalls for a plug of chewing tobacco. While I drank the moonshine he worked up a spit.

One of the curs came too close; the old man puckered up and got him in the eye with a snap shot. The dog howled and ran away. "Time to talk," the old man announced. "Talk plain and not too long."

I explained about Luke, the mail order bride; how I came to be taking Luke's place. The old man chewed and spat, holding the 44-40 across his bony knees. "That's the first part of it," I went on. "The second part—why I'm here—is a man named Malachi Fallon."

The old man spoke around his wad of wet tobacco. "That's only why you think you're here. You're here because I let you be here. Zachariah Eldredge is who I am.

I said I was pleased to make his acquaintance.

"Don't be," he said.

"This man Fallon rode out this way," I said. "He asked for the Eldredge place by name, so it's no guess. The boy there is wearing Fallon's hat."

30

"You calling Willy a thief?"

I shook my head. "Fallon rode out this way with four men. When he got back to town he was missing one man, one hat. Later a farmer brought in the fourth man with a bullet through his head."

"Don't say," Zack Eldredge remarked, not looking too interested.

"You wouldn't want to tell me what Fallon was doing out here?" I was used to most all kinds of bad liquor, but that Eldredge moonshine buzzed in my head.

"Wouldn't and couldn't," the old man declared hard and flat. "Don't know the man. Don't want to know him. The same goes for you."

I never saw a man more disinclined to help the law of the land. Zack Eldredge had a way of making everything he said sound final, like Moses setting the Israelites straight on this and that. It must have worked well with all his murderous kinfolk because he was still boss in his old age, but it might not be enough to stop Malachi Fallon. Neither man knew how dangerous the other could be, so there wouldn't be any backing off.

I told the old man I didn't want any more whiskey.

"Then I'll take a drink," he announced. He wouldn't drink with me; now it was all right to drink by himself.

"Maybe Fallon and his men threatened you," I said. "They got tough and you killed one of the gunslingers. No jury can fault you for that."

Laughing didn't come easy to the old mountaineer. The laugh started with a rasping chuckle in the back of his throat; it ended with a few short barks. He glared at me with fierce red eyes. "Nobody threatens an Eldredge," he said. "You seen my boys. You think they look threatened?"

I had to admit they didn't look worried. I tried to tell him that killing Fallon's gunman was just the beginning. I said Fallon could come back with forty men. Once more I tried to get him to answer the big question: what was Malachi Fallon doing in Salter City?

"Time's up," Zack Eldredge said. "No more questions, no more talk. Now you climb back on that horse and don't you ever come back. You tend to your business and we'll tend to ours. This Fallon could be our business. Not for you to ask and not for me to say. Since you seem to know all about him, suppose you carry a message. Zachariah Eldredge don't give a damn for four, nor forty, nor four hundred hired gunmen. The next man steps on my land gets buried where he falls. That includes you."

I don't know what made me turn my head, but when I did turn it I saw the yellow-haired girl watching me from inside the door of the old man's cabin. One thing she didn't look like was an Eldredge. She looked no more like the other female scarecrows than a racehorse does a mule. Even in a crowd of pretty big city women she would have stood out; there on the Eldredge place she didn't belong at all; and the green silk dress she wore cost enough to keep all her kinfolk in whiskey and bullets for a year.

The old man saw where I was looking. "Sally," he roared. "You girl—shut that door."

I got up off the nail keg where I was sitting. The old man's fierce eyes defied me to ask any more questions. "You change your mind about Fallon, come and see me," I said.

"Fetch his horse," Eldredge roared to the boy. "Give him back his guns, then the rest of you walk him off the property."

On the way back to the road I asked the boy Willy if he'd let me buy back Fallon's hat. "Give you a dollar for it," I said. "Got a hole in it or I'd offer you more."

Willy cracked his long-jawed face in a foxy grin. "Grampaw would want for me to get more than that. It's a nice hat. Two dollars worth of nice. Hole don't hardly show a-tall."

I gave him the two dollars and got Fallon's hat. Out on the road I put spurs to the horse and turned back toward town. "Hey, ain't you even going to try it on?" Willy called after me.

CHAPTER FOUR

The bitter taste of the Eldredge moonshine was in my mouth all the way back to Salter City. It was getting dark when I got there and, not being Saturday night, the town was quiet. The brightest light belonged to the town's only saloon; the saloon was quiet too. The old fella who ran the restaurant had hung out the Closed sign, but when he saw it was me, he unbolted the door.

"Wouldn't do it for nobody but you, Sheriff," he told me.

He thought that entitled him to ask questions. In a one-horse town with one restaurant you learn not to set the cook against you. I turned the questions aside and told him to fry a steak and charge it to Luke.

While the steak was cooking I got confidential; the cook liked that. I jerked my head toward the street. "Anything interesting happen while I been gone?" I asked him. There was no need to explain my meaning; the whole town was buzzing about Fallon and his interest in the Eldredges.

The door was bolted and the place was empty except for us, but the cook looked around and lowered his voice when he spoke. "One of them fellas came over to get food about the time you rode out. You'd think he was in some big city, the way he bitched about my cooking. I guess they ate it, though, because he was over here a while ago for more."

I started to eat my steak. "Then they're still at the hotel?" I said.

"One of them rode out about an hour after you left," the cook said. "Took the north road and was in an awful hurry. Where do you figure he went to?"

"Don't know," I said. The reason Fallon was in town was still a puzzle, but now I had one or two of the pieces. Somehow Fallon and the girl called Sally were tied in together. It made no sense for Fallon to be interested in any other Eldredge. It had to be the girl. It was just as plain that Sally Eldredge hadn't always lived near Salter City. Whatever it was, it was important enough to bring

36

Malachi Fallon all the way to the badlands of south Texas.

I went over to the hotel and went upstairs without speaking to the clerk. The same hard case opened the door, and he was as pleased to see me as he'd been the first time. But there was no smart talk, and I was glad of that. It had been kind of a long day for me, and I was about ready to knock out his front teeth with a gun barrel if he started bad-mouthing me again.

"The sheriff," he said over his shoulder to Fallon.

"Let him in, Dutch," Fallon called out, sounding a bit drunk. "No, better ask him what he wants."

"What do you want?" Dutch asked, looking at the hat I held in my left hand. The hole in the hat got as much attention as the hat itself.

I grinned at Dutch. "Tell Fallon I found his hat."

I couldn't see Fallon because the gunman was blocking the door. "Take the hat, Dutch, and give the sheriff a dollar. Tell him thanks for me."

Fallon was having a good time, or making out that he was. "Naw, that isn't polite. Let the sheriff in."

The window was closed and the room stank of cigar smoke and whiskey. Nothing else had changed except that Fallon was more bleary-eyed than usual. Still on the bed, a glass in his hand, he didn't look as good-humored as he sounded. Fallon's crinkly ginger hair was mussed and he made a big to-do about combing it back with his fingers.

"Got to show respect for the law," he told the two gunslingers.

That started them laughing.

Fallon snapped his fingers and pretended to frown. "None of that, boys," he said. "Fetch the sheriff a chair, Clem. You, Dutch, you fix the sheriff a drink."

I'll say one thing for Fallon: he drank a good brand of whiskey. That's all I could say for him. The slack-mouth son of a bitch pointed to his own glass, and Dutch filled it. Spilling some of the whiskey, Fallon raised his glass and said, "Your good health, sir."

"You want your hat?" I enquired, putting my finger through the hole in the crown.

"No," Fallon said. "It's got a hole in it. Hope you didn't go to too much trouble to get it."

There was no hole in my hat, so I was able to lie. "No trouble," I said. "By the way, Sally sends her regards." I tossed the hat onto the bed and turned toward the door.

"Hey, wait a minute," Fallon said, putting his big bare feet on the floor. "Slow down there."

"Slow down for what?"

"You haven't finished your drink."

I said I had.

"Then have another," Fallon said. "Don't tell me it isn't good—it's the best."

Dutch filled the glass and I sat down. "Sally sends regards, is that it?" Fallon said. "Sally a good friend of yours?"

"Pretty good," I answered.

"You're a liar," Fallon said quietly. "I bet you don't even know what she looks like."

I said I knew what she looked like. I said I liked everything about Sally.

Fallon watched me carefully, trying to size me up. "That kind of talk could get you in trouble," he said. "Maybe you better forget about Sally."

The bluff was working, but I still didn't have any answers. "That'd be kind of hard to do," I said. "A lady in distress, as the fella said. Being sheriff, it's my job to help her every way I know how."

Fallon sidetracked for a while. He tried to sound easy, maybe even friendly, but I knew his crooked lawyer's brain was working hard to figure me out. I figured he would try the soft talk first, then the threats. He pulled his rubbery lips back in what was supposed to pass for a smile. It looked more like a cowardly vicious dog trying to get up enough nerve to bite somebody.

"You haven't been sheriff long, have you?" Fallon said.

I knew he'd been checking around town. "Not long," I said.

"Sort of temporary, the way I hear it," Fallon stated. "That means you'll be looking for another job. How'd you like to work for me?"

"Doing what?"

"What I tell you. That's what Clem and Dutch do. They don't ask the reasons—they just do it. They're good boys. They'd gun you in a wink if I said so."

"Maybe not," I said. "Mike did what he was told and he's dead. Any time Dutch and Clem want to try . . . You too, Fallon."

"That's what I like, a man with guts," Fallon said. "You want to work for me or not?"

"Not," I said.

Trying again while he bit off the end of a cigar and dipped it in his whiskey, Fallon asked me how I'd like a soft law job up in Pecos County. "I could fix it," he said. Dutch and Clem smiled. "People listen to me up there. People all over listen to me when I talk. That kind of deal sound good to you?"

I pretended to think about it. "Maybe," I said. "Depends what I'd have to do."

"That's the good part," Fallon told me. "You don't have to do a thing."

I helped myself to more whiskey, and Fallon seemed to take that as a good sign. "Drink up," he said.

"About Sally . . ." I began.

"That's it," Fallon said. "I was coming to Sally. You don't do a thing about Sally. I'm counting on you to take that job in Pecos County."

"Sure," I said.

"All right then, here it is," Fallon. "You ever hear of Big Sam Thornton? I guess everybody in Texas has. Well, sir, this Sally is Mrs. Sam Thornton of New Orleans. It seems that Mr. and Mrs. Thornton had a disagreement about something and Mrs. Sam decided to light out for home. Home is here on the Eldredge place. You know how married folks fight, Sheriff, except that it's a bit more com-

40

plicated than that. Mr. Thornton wants his pretty young wife back, but she doesn't want to go. That's what she thinks, being a woman. Mr. Thornton doesn't like that. That's why I'm here with the boys, to sort of persuade her . . . "

Fallon talked on, enjoying his own windy statements. I was thinking about Big Sam Thornton. Like Fallon said, everybody in Texas knew who Sam Thornton was. Sam was a nice fella all right, maybe the meanest outlaw Texas ever produced, and that was saying something. Sam and his wild bunch still called themselves guerillas long after the War was over, but folks didn't get too excited about the bank robbing and train wrecking. They didn't get their backs up until one night Sam and his boys herded a farmer, his wife and four kids into a barn, barred the door and set the place on fire. After that there was no amnesty for Thornton, no place he could hide—not in Texas. After he ran away from Texas he robbed and murdered in Kansas and Oklahoma. Chased out of there, he holed up in Louisiana, the only state without an extradition law. In the ten years since he'd stopped running from the law in three states, Thornton had become something of a leading citizen in New Orleans, meaning that now he was rich and powerful enough to hire other men to do his killing for him. Powerful enough to get men like Fallon to jump when he cracked the whip. . . .

"Mr. Thornton wants his wife back," Fallon was telling me. "He won't take no."

"Maybe he should come himself," I said, laying

down my glass. Now the pieces of the puzzle were all together. Thornton couldn't come back to Texas or they'd hang him. It figured that Fallon was tied in to Thornton from the old days. Maybe Thornton had something dirty on Fallon, or maybe the price was right. It was well known that Thornton had a way of reaching out from his big house in New Orleans and getting what he wanted.

"Course they'd hang him if he did," I said. "Not even President Garfield could pardon him for what he did, the dirty child-killing son of a bitch!"

"Hold it, boys," Fallon said quickly. To me he said, "You're talking crazy. What you're saying is a pack of rotten lies. Sure Mr. Thornton did some wild things in his time, but, I swear, he had nothing to do with killing that farmer's family. There never was any proof of that. I suppose you didn't know Mr. Thornton has a standing reward of ten thousand dollars for the real killers. One of these days Mr. Thornton is going to clear his name in this state."

His own words were getting Fallon worked up. I must have looked doubtful because he made one last try to convince me that Big Sam Thornton was a man wronged. He shook his head sorrowfully, surprised at me for thinking he was a bad fella. "You don't think I'd be helping Sam Thornton if I thought for a minute those charges were true. Oh, for God's sake!"

The big man from Pecos County, the man who ran his own candidates and had connections everywhere, had asked me a question. "I think you'd do

42

just about anything, Fallon. Look what you're doing now."

In a way, I hoped the two gunmen would try to finish me then and there. If there had been three of them I might not have been so eager. But I knew I could handle these two and then turn my gun on Fallon. No doubt Sam Thornton wouldn't give up on his pretty yellow-haired runaway wife, but I figured he might have trouble finding another go-between like Fallon.

Fallon took the insult without blowing up. Maybe he knew what I had in mind. He took a deep breath and when he let it out his rubbery lips vibrated like a horse blowing wind. Rubbing the side of his head like a man tired out with arguing, he said, "You got a bad mouth—what is it?—Carmody. Maybe that comes from pushing these yokels around. Maybe you think you're good with that gun of yours. Maybe you are. Doesn't mean a thing, not to me. You get in my way—really get in my way—and I'll mash you like a bug."

It was that bug talk that got me. A man can threaten to kill me, and I don't mind. Let him try. Then let him die trying. What Fallon had just said left absolutely no room for me to back off. Without knowing it—he had no way of knowing me—Fallon had made the last big mistake of his life.

I got up and stood easy, still hoping the gunmen would move without Fallon's say-so. When they didn't I spoke my piece: "You may start the trouble here, but I'll finish it. You think because you have the money to hire guns you can walk in here and take a woman doesn't want to be taken. You're the lawyer, you figure what charge that is. It won't get to court because I'll kill you. Maybe you'll try to kill me first, but we'll see who gets killed."

Fallon stopped rubbing his head and looked at me. "All right, I'm shaking in my boots. Just tell me one thing—why? You're no lawman and you know it. You don't even know the girl and it isn't your town—so why? Don't tell me you're a friend of lost ladies, pretty or otherwise. You're not the type."

"You're one reason," I told him. "You wouldn't understand the rest."

"You can't win," Fallon said as I backed out of the room.

Going back to the jail I had to admit that Fallon might be right. Maybe Fallon didn't understand my reasons for taking a stand, and maybe I didn't understand all of them myself. But there I was in the middle of something that wasn't rightly my business.

Talking to myself isn't one of my habits; now I said: "Carmody, however did you manage to live so long?"

CHAPTER FIVE

I was bunking in Luke's cell, the one with an Indian rug on the stone floor and pictures of his mail-order sweetheart tacked to a board that hung on the back wall. Luke, being the thrifty type, didn't believe in wasting his easy-earned money on hotel rooms when there was a nice clean jail for the taking. There were some chains set into the wall out back where he shackled the more troublesome drunks on Saturday nights. I don't know what Luke would have done if he had a real dangerous or important prisoner on his hands; likely as not, the problem would never come up.

I didn't think Fallon would try to get me in the jail if he hadn't tried it outside. Doing things the underhand way was more Fallon's style. A fixer and a crook, he wouldn't go against the law head-on unless there was no other way. I wondered if I'd done right in not killing him and letting the game go on from there. Maybe I hadn't killed him because of Luke. Luke wouldn't be the one to pull the trigger, but ten to one Fallon's political cronies had enough weight with the Governor to finish Luke as a county sheriff. I don't mind telling you, I cursed Cousin Luke quietly and for some time.

After I barred the jail door I loaded that monster goose-gun and laid it on the floor beside the Winchester. The town was quiet, and by the time I drank all the whiskey I wanted there were no sounds at all. For a long time I lay awake trying to figure how I'd handle the situation. After seeing Sally Eldredge, I didn't blame Sam Thornton for wanting her back. But Sally didn't want to go and Sam, being somewhat crazy, wouldn't take no for an answer. Maybe Sally Eldredge thought she was safe surrounded by her gun-happy kinfolk; I knew better. In the end, the Eldredges would be no match for Thornton's hired killers. There were only so many Eldredges, but in Texas alone Thornton, working through Fallon, could hire enough professional gunslingers to make a small army. Anxious to avoid a stink that would go far beyond Salter City, Fallon would try the crooked way first. But when the chips were down, Fallon would do what he was told. I didn't know what Thornton

46

had on Fallon. It could be something as simple as letting him live.

Sometimes when you sleep on something you have the answer when you wake up. I didn't. The wound in my side looked to be healing up, and that was the only good news I had on that particular morning. The sun was just warming up the dust when I unbarred the jail door and took a look at my Goddamned town.

The sun was up full and hot by the time I finished the second cigarette. I didn't want to walk in on any surprises when I got back, so I locked up the jail and took the key with me to the eating place run by the old man. "Better just have the fried eggs," he told me when I said ham and eggs. "The ham don't look cured right to me. I'll just chop it up and dump it in the pea soup. That ought to do it."

Cracked into bacon fat, the eggs began to sizzle. The old man made good coffee and the first cup burned away some of my sour mood. "I guess you know this town pretty good," I said. "Know any likely fellas would like to hire on as deputies?"

The old man turned the eggs and came back with the coffee pot. He was bright enough for an old man who had spent his life frying eggs. "I'd have to say no," he said. "A couple of days ago I'd say yes. Times are bad hereabouts, money scarce. A couple of days ago you'd be knee deep in deputies. Not now, I reckon. Talk's been going round since that gunman got himself killed by the Eldredges. What do you think?"

I finished my eggs and got up. "I think you ought to send Fallon some of that pea soup. Do the same for Zachariah Eldredge. If you hear of any would-be deputies let me know."

On this morning, at least, Fallon wasn't an early riser. I wondered how long it would take his gunman to get back to town. My guess was that he was heading for the nearest telegraph office; that would be where the railroad bent south, about a two-day ride from Salter City. That would be the obvious thing to do. But it was just possible, too, that Fallon hadn't brought all his men into town.

Thinking about that took me down to the livery stable. The two boys who worked there were having a stand-up breakfast of fried bread and buttermilk. No, sir, they told me, nobody had come in and put up horses during the night. One kid was talky and the other wasn't. They looked like brothers, the mouthy one about sixteen, the quiet one a year younger.

"You don't have to do that," the talky brother said when I flipped a silver dollar between them.

The quiet one picked it up; only my badge kept him from testing it with his teeth. "Sure he does," he said. "We're orphans—remember?"

"You two got names?" I asked them.

They told me. Finley was the one who talked; his brother was Todd. I don't think Todd was ready to settle down to a life of fried bread and buttermilk. The boy looked pinched in the face. "That other dollar should be for helping you with

48

the dead man," he told me. "Wanting us to tell you things we see ought to be worth another dollar."

Finley looked embarrassed. "Don't mind him," he said. "All he thinks about is money."

I went back to the sheriff's office and, for want of something better to do, looked through the sheaf of wanted posters on the spike. I had to grin at some of the faces in the pile; most of them I didn't know. I was reading about some old murderer called Baldy Fitch when I heard loud voices out in the street.

Fallon, looking all spruced up in a change of suits, was out there talking to the mayor. I don't think it was a salaried job, being mayor of Salter City, but that's what they called Dunstan, the man who didn't get along so good with Luke. It was hot and quiet in the street, and I could hear every word Fallon let go.

Fallon looked my way when I stepped out of the jail door. Then he looked away and put his arm around Mayor Dunstan's shoulder and said again that, in his opinion, Salter City looked to be a town with possibilities. Dunstan, a fat, sour man, wanted to believe what Fallon was saying, but even he looked doubtful.

Fallon shoveled some more bullshit. Even for a flannelmouth like him it was hard to work up a sweat about a forgotten hole like Salter City, but he did his best. The cattle business wasn't good and any fool could see it wasn't likely to be, so Fallon stayed away from that. "The finest climate in the world," Fallon said vaguely, digging Dunstan in the ribs. The Mayor wasn't the rib-digging sort, but, coming from Fallon, he liked it. "Good location too," Fallon went on. "Water's a bit scarce but we'll face that problem when we come to it. I'd say the folks in this town have enough get-up-and-go to tackle any problem. Yes, sir, Mr. Mayor, I think I can safely tell my friends up north that Salter City has possibilities."

Mayor Dunstan, no doubt seeing a flow of money into his broken-down bank, wanted to hear everything Fallon had to say. Especially he wanted to hear what in hell Fallon had in mind.

"A little early for that, Mr. Mayor," Fallon said. "Sort of confidential, if you know what I mean. If it got out before the right moment, other towns would come clamoring for attention. Can't let that happen, can we?"

I couldn't hear what Dunstan was saying, but I knew what it was. He was a businessman and he understood. "A little talk later in your office," Fallon suggested.

Dunstan nodded confidentially.

I figured why not. "Morning, Sheriff," Fallon called out when I stepped into the street. "Sure is a fine morning."

Fallon was in real good humor; maybe he thought he knew how to handle me.

Dunstan didn't even nod at me. "What are you fixing to do, Fallon?" I asked. "Build a hotel for consumption cases? Sure is a fine climate for that."

Mayor Dunstan glowered at me. "We were having a private conversation," he protested. "Nothing to do with you. This is business."

The way I butted in didn't bother Fallon. His two gunslingers were watching from the hotel porch. I guess Fallon felt safe enough; in command of the situation, as the military fellas say when things are going good.

Fallon laughed, making me out to be a card. "That's a good one, Sheriff," he told me. "A hotel for consumption cases! Not a bad idea if the railroad ever runs a line south."

Dunstan said, "I said this was a private conversation."

I grinned at him. "Not the way Fallon shouts."

"Mister Fallon to you," Dunstan blustered. "You don't have any better manners than your cousin."

Men like Dunstan can say things like that without getting a gun barrel laid across their skulls. They're old and fat, more like old women than anything else, and that makes them safe.

"Poor bringing up, I guess," was all I said to Dunstan.

"Show some respect," Dunstan said. Every big ear in town was turned our way, so Dunstan said it again.

"All right," I said to Dunstan. "You're the businessman. You do the talking. This new business Mister Fallon . . ."

"No need to mister me," Fallon said. "Malachi Fallon's plain as an old shoe. Call me anything you like. Just don't keep me out of the gravy."

"Suppose you ask Fallon about the Eldredges," I told Dunstan. "I guess you know about the Eldredges, Mr. Mayor?"

This time Dunstan looked uncomfortable; more uncomfortable than he did usually, I mean. "I'm not about to ask Mr. Fallon anything," he said. "Mr. Fallon is a man who is known to me by reputation."

"Loved by one and all," I said.

Fallon was all good nature. "You know, Sheriff Carmody, if I didn't know better I'd say you didn't like me."

"Why don't you ask him?" I asked Dunstan.

"Certainly not," Dunstan said, sweating in the fierce heat. He turned to Fallon. "You want to have that talk now, Mr. Fallon?"

Dunstan was madder than hell at me and Fallon, always a friend of the plain man, took up for me. He poked the mayor in the ribs again, and winked. "Don't mind the sheriff," he said. "Wouldn't be a good lawman if he didn't suspect everybody came to town, even me. We'll have that talk later, if you don't mind. I hope you got some good whiskey. To celebrate, I mean."

I don't think Mayor Dunstan ever had a drink in his life, but he managed a good-fella smile. "It's an honor to have you in Salter City, Mr. Fallon. And now good morning."

Fallon smiled at Dunstan's back and then he smiled at me. He wasn't wearing his bullet-holed hat and sweat trickled out of his crinkly hair and ran into his eyes. He wiped it away with a hand-

52

kerchief, then stuffed the handkerchief into his sleeve.

"How did I do?" he asked in a low voice.

"You did good," I said. "Dunstan bit hard but you didn't yank on the line. That was good, you slimy son of a bitch."

"Too late to kill me," Fallon said.

"Maybe not," I said.

"I think you should have done it yesterday. Now it's too late. Soon it'll be later than that."

"Don't count on it, Fallon."

Fallon, maybe not so sure for a moment, looked to see if the two gunslingers were backing his mouth with their guns. They were.

"You know what I count on, Carmody?" Fallon answered his own question. "Money and then some more money. More money on top of that. And so on. I can tap one bank that never runs dry. Why don't you get to thinking the same way? Start sucking on that hind tit before the rush starts. Man, don't you see? No one man can go against the power of money."

I wiped the sweat off my own face and thought it was funny, me and Fallon talking in low voices while all the big ears in town strained to hear what we were saying. Fallon, I guess, had thought a lot about the power of money, as he called it. So had I, but not in quite the same way.

"You could be wrong this once," I said. Kind of a fool thing it was to say, but I said it. Maybe I sounded a bit lame. So would you, then and there.

"Never been wrong except those two times I ran

for office," Fallon said. He wiped his face again. He raised his hand to take off his hat, then remembered it wasn't there.

"That proves it," I said.

"Proves I didn't spread enough money around," Fallon said. "This time I will. It isn't my money, so I can heap it on with a trowel. I tell you, Carmody, I'm going to turn this whole town against you. First with promises and then with money, if I have to. The money is only the start, you understand. Usually it's the start and the finish." Fallon did a take-off on Mayor Dunstan's whiny voice. "You want to have a little talk?"

"Not just yet," I said.

CHAPTER SIX

That night Fallon gave a party at the hotel. I wasn't invited, but I guess that was an oversight. Anyway, I don't know that sheriffs get invited too much. People figure sheriffs just naturally show up at parties. They don't get invited, but nobody keeps them out when they come to bend their heads over the punch bowl.

Killing Fallon was still a good idea—a useful idea, anyway—but it came to me that it would be a better idea if Sally Eldredge took her pretty self far away from Salter City. The more I thought about it, the better it looked. With the chair pulled close to the door of the jail where I could see things, getting Sally gone from Salter City looked better all the time. The thought came to me, as thoughts do, while I was building a smoke. It wasn't important enough to make my hand shake, but it was worth thinking about. Here and there, trying to keep busy, watching the town, it kept coming back all through the day. With Sally gone Fallon would go too. It was a nice idea, simple as hell. Sally would go and Fallon would go, leaving me with nothing better to do but wait for Luke to get back. I liked the idea. Luke would bring his new bride back, maybe let me kiss her in a cousinly way, and then, having done that, I would take the money Luke owed me and head for the border. It would be fine, I thought, to wipe the dust of Salter City off my scarred boots.

I liked the idea so much I decided to do something about it the first chance I got. When that chance would come I had no notion. Sally with the yellow hair and the body to think about wasn't making the trouble—Fallon was making the trouble and would always make some kind of trouble— but that wasn't the point. With Sally gone, the trouble gone with her, it would be hard not to kill Fallon to make things tidy. There would be times, I guess, when I was feeling mean and thought about it, when I would kick myself for not killing Malachi Fallon on general principles. I knew the feeling would pass.

How to talk Sally Eldredge into wiping the dust of Salter City off her shoes was what I was thinking about, early that evening, when I heard the music over at the hotel. It was the first music Salter City had heard for a dog's age. I thought one thing Salter City needed was more music. Of all the miserable towns I'd been in, Salter City needed music more than any other. I finished the drink I was drinking, poured another, and listened to the music.

I didn't know how I'd get Sally out of Salter City. That was what I wanted to do, and I didn't know how to do it. A girl with kinfolk not as numerous, not as trigger-happy, could be approached and asked in a reasonable way. Doing that, with all the Eldredges pointing guns at me, was something I hadn't thought out yet.

Maybe all that figuring had left me a little drunk.

I corked the bottle and left it on the desk and went to the door. The single saloon looked much the same; all the whoop-dee-do was at the hotel. The music sounded like a mechanical harp being interfered with by a fiddle and banjo. A horn joined in, or tried to, while I stood there and listened. None of it was good, but it didn't have to be. I knew it had to be Malachi Fallon laying on some of Big Sam Thornton's money with a trowel.

I gave it a while. It was dark, not long so, and no party I ever knew got going till the first empty bottles were knocked over by somebody setting down the second empty bottles. I gave it a while, still thinking about Sally Eldredge in the same, and different, ways. It was easy to think about Sally.

57

I locked the jail and walked down to the livery stable. There was a lantern burning out front under the sign. I went in and the talky kid was asleep in his blanket on a heap of straw. The one called Todd was huddled up close to a lamp reading a book. He put his finger in the book to mark his place and asked me which one I thought was the smartest—Harriman or Gould?

"Harriman," I said.

"I wonder," the kid said.

No, he told me finally, no strange horses had been put up. It was still the same as before.

I didn't want to get into an argument about Jay Gould, so I walked down to the hotel.

In the sad old days when Salter City got started, the man who built the hotel included a ballroom. It wasn't much of a hotel, not much of a ballroom either, but now they had moved the dust around and opened it up. The ballroom opened off the lobby and the clockwork harp and the other noisemakers were banging away when I went in. All the notes were sour, but I guess I was sourer than most, because the clerk turned his face grim when I went in.

It wasn't much of a crowd, but then no crowd in Salter City would be much of a crowd. The whole town plus all the locals who scratched out a living wouldn't make much of a crowd. I winked at the clerk and made my way into the ballroom.

People were dancing like people who hadn't paid for their liquor. Two young fellas I didn't know were behind a makeshift bar, planks laid across trestles, pouring as fast as they could move the bottles. Other gents, not wanting to wait, were helping themselves to the free whiskey. A punch bowl for the ladies stood on a table by itself.

In honor of the occasion, whatever it was, Mayor Dunstan was dipping that ladle into the punch bowl. A bitter-faced woman who could only be his wife was waiting for him to fill her glass. Maybe she was naturally bitter and maybe being married to Mayor Dunstan helped.

I didn't look for Fallon, I looked for his two gunslingers and any others who might have arrived. They were there all right, still just the two of them, and so was Fallon. The two gunmen saw me right away, but Fallon was too busy with a soft-faced fat woman to give me more than a quick look.

Mayor Dunstan spilled some of his wife's punch when he saw me. I smiled at him and went to the bar and let one of the bartenders pour me a drink. I tasted the free whiskey. It was about average. Every town has good whiskey, if you dip down to pay for it, but Fallon hadn't dipped down that far. It was a fool thought at the time, but I wondered how much Fallon cheated on his bills to Sam Thornton.

Fallon was still jollying the fat woman. Her husband, fat like herself but with nowhere like the muscles, came up and stood beside them, waiting for the big man from up Pecos County way to say hello.

Fallon didn't just say hello. He dug the fat gent

in the ribs and bear-hugged him. I guess the timid fat gent was the town carpenter and part-time coffin maker. I sort of recalled who he was; he looked different without his apron.

Fallon chucked the fat woman under the chin and turned to look at me. With all that noise, I don't know how he knew I was there. Not wanting to lose Fallon's attention, the fat woman grabbed at his arm. Fallon squeezed her high on the arm and the fat woman darted a look at her husband and giggled.

"You're awful, Mr. Fallon," she said.

Fallon, looking at me, told the fat woman to dance with her husband. The fat woman didn't like that, not much anyway.

"You can have this one, Mr. Ryker," Fallon warned the fat woman's husband. He winked at the carpenter. The carpenter winked back and made a bold attempt, maybe his first, to sweep his fat wife into the tangle of a fast waltz.

"You're drinking—good," Fallon said to me. "How d'you like the party?" He spoke over his shoulder while he went to the bar and came back with a full glass.

"It's a good party," he said.

"You forgot to invite Sally Eldredge," I said.

Fallon answered after he bit into his drink. "Wrong, I did invite them," he said. "Sally and all the Eldredges. Maybe they'll show up later."

"You won't like it if they do."

"They won't show up."

Another swallow killed Fallon's drink. At the far

end of the dusty ballroom, the mechanical harp made a grinding noise, as if it needed oil. The live musicians played louder to cover it up. They were a game trio, those three live musicians; the horn player worked hardest of all. The harp twanged away the same as before; after a while the grinding grew quieter, then faded away.

Fallon said: "Drink up and enjoy the party." He kept his voice down. "I decided not to build the hotel for lungers, Carmody." He hiccuped and rubbed his rubbery mouth with the back of his hand. "A railroad south to Mexico is what this town needs."

Never in my life had I met a man with so much crook to his character. All crook was what Malachi Fallon was; no mistake about it. I looked across the ballroom at his two gunslingers looking sour because they didn't have drinks in their hands.

"South to Mexico with the railroad. I haven't decided which line yet." Fallon grabbed at my glass and I let him have it.

He came back and handed me the glass. "How's that for service?" he asked.

"Not just a spurline," I said, thinking what a son of a bitch this man was. "A real through line to Mexico."

Mayor Dunstan, still lumbering near the punch bowl, was trying to listen. Fallon raised his voice so he could be heard. "I tell you, Sheriff Carmody, this is going to be one lively town before long."

I swallowed my drink. "Livelier than you think,

friend. You still got time to back off. Be the smart man they say you are—back off."

My voice was quieter than Fallon's.

"Money for everybody," Fallon said so everybody could hear him. Bringing his voice down again, he said: "For you too, Carmody."

"You keep saying that, Fallon."

"Not much longer, Carmody. Think about it while you got the chance. I'm bringing the railroad south—that's official as of tonight—so that makes me as popular as the man who invented money the first time."

I gave Fallon my empty glass. "You're not going to leave so early," he said, twisting his face into a satisfied smile. "Why, man, the party's just getting started. Stay a while and watch me work."

I gave him a mean grin. "Not just a railroad?" I asked him. "That's too modest for a man like Malachi Fallon. What else?"

Suddenly I realized that Fallon had nothing personal against me. I was just somebody in his way; somebody to get got out of the way. Maybe he really didn't know that some people, a few, won't budge when they make up their minds to stay still.

"You think of something I haven't thought of and I'll promise that too," Fallon said. "You'll say no, maybe you'll say no, but I'm the one they'll believe. Makes you wonder, doesn't it?"

Mayor Dunstan had gone up to the stage and was telling the musicians to keep quiet. The three noisemakers did what they were told; the harp, clockworked as it was, went on making noise.

Mayor Dunstan looked like he wanted to kick the harp to death. I don't think he was cursing, but he looked like he was. People laughed and yelled and the hotel clerk came running.

The clerk did something to the harp; it twanged to a halt. Fallon turned to me while Mayor Dunstan was calling for quiet. "You can't stop me, Carmody," he said. "Don't be foolish, don't try."

I shrugged. Dunstan, red-faced, was calling on Fallon to get up there and make a speech. I didn't want to listen to Fallon's speech. I thought I knew what it would be like. Lies and more lies, all the bullshit they wanted to hear.

The two gunslingers watched me go out.

I was running low on whiskey, so I snagged a bottle from the bar and went back to the jail. That would please Mayor Dunstan no end. Fallon was turning the town against me, and it wasn't hard to do. Buying off the town with promises, free whiskey and maybe a little money scattered about was Fallon's way of taking out insurance. If Fallon had been a wild man like his boss, Thornton, he would have ridden into Salter City with all the gunmen it took to blast the Eldredges to kingdom come; then take the girl and hightail it back to Louisiana. And maybe that was Big Sam Thornton's first thought. But Fallon wanted to stay in business after the trouble was over. It could even be that Fallon had checked to see who the sheriff was in Salter City. Maybe Fallon knew Cousin Luke by reputation; knowing the easy-to-buy sheriff Luke was would make the whole job seem easier.

My brain was working too hard, and I gave it a rest. I drank Fallon's whiskey and thought about Sally Eldredge, but not in a business way. That was a sure sign that I was getting well. Maybe other men can take the time to think about women when they're getting over slow-healing bullet wounds; not me. Now I was ready to think about women, about one woman. The short time I'd been in Salter City hadn't turned up any other woman worth clapping a saddle on.

The party over at the hotel was going good. Nobody could say it sounded like a wild party—Salter City was no kind of a wild town—but it was probably the only party the town had seen for some time.

I don't know how much time had passed since I took the bottle and left, maybe two hours, something like that, when I heard voices coming across the street. I got up and closed the door but didn't bar it. I moved the chair some distance from the desk and sat in it with Luke's goose-gun across my knee. Anybody with nerve enough to kick open the door and shoot at where I usually sat would be making a small mistake. And a blast from the goose-gun would make them sorry for it. Naturally I didn't think it would come to that, not yet; I was just being careful.

The voices stopped before they reached the jail. I dropped a cigarette stub on the floor and stepped on it. Mayor Dunstan spoke first. "Are you in there, Sheriff?"

"No place else," I yelled back. "Come on in."

Dunstan didn't come in first; a big brute of a man I knew to be the town blacksmith opened the door. I think his name was Bullock, and it suited him. He'd been drinking or dancing or both; it seemed funny that a man who worked in heat all the time in a hot country should sweat so much. The few strands of blond hair left on his bullet head were plastered down with sweat; and there were widening stains under both arms of his black wool suit.

I grinned at him. "Where's Dunstan?" I asked.

The blacksmith pushed the door open all the way, and Dunstan came in, followed by five men. I knew two of them by sight. I didn't know the others, but they were all the same breed: small town storekeepers and businessmen with the smell of money in their noses. They didn't have anything to say; the Mayor was the man with the mouth.

"Evening, Mayor. Evening, gents," I told them in a friendly enough tone. I had nothing against the sons of bitches; I had nothing for them either. Money smells just as sweet in my nose, but that doesn't make me grub for it. Work hard maybe while I'm planning to take it—scheme hard if I have to—but grubbing for it is something I'd rather not do.

It hurt Dunstan to be polite to me. The banker, being a banker, was the kind of man to make a sour face at a poor man's hello, then run to wash the dust off a rich man's boots with his own spit.

Dunstan harrumped in the back of his throat. That's the word for the noise he made. "Evening,

'Sheriff," he said at last through a mouth as puckered as a dog's rear-end in an alkali bed.

Those stiff-collared musty-suited storekeepers turned me mean. Maybe in the whole world there was one storekeeping man with enough guts to be called a real man. I had never met such a man. "Evening, gents," I said again.

They mumbled back, some not liking me, some maybe even hating me because I was an obstacle that had to be moved, or climbed over, before they could get to the money. The money they thought was on the way—Fallon's money. They hadn't said a word yet, but I knew they were moving while Fallon sat back at the hotel and pulled the strings.

From where I sat, the goose-gun making the storekeepers nervous, Fallon didn't look so bad. Sure he was a doublecrosser and a go-between and an all-round son of a bordertown whore. He didn't try hard to be anything else.

Only the big blacksmith wasn't nervous with me. Dunstan was more nervous than the others, but then he'd been talking to Fallon. I wondered if he'd dipped into the punch bowl just once in his life before he got up enough nerve to tell me to quit.

That's what he was going to tell me. I was feeling mean, and I thought that was funny.

CHAPTER SEVEN

Before he spoke Dunstan made sure the blacksmith hadn't disappeared in a pool of sweat. Bullock, the blacksmith, was the man closer to me
than anybody else. Bullock stood to one side so
that Dunstan could see when he talked. Dunstan
was back a ways and the storekeepers, taking no
chances, were herded together inside the open
door.

"We want to talk to you, Carmody," Dunstan
began, puckering and unpuckering his womanish
lips. And they were womanish lips, maybe spoiled
baby lips. "It's time for a talk," Dunstan went on.

I crossed my knees the other way and you know how things happen when you move around trying to get comfortable. Of course I didn't move my knees so the muzzle of the goose-gun was staring Dunstan in the face when he started again.

Like hell I didn't!

At first, Dunstan was like a rabbit looking at a snake. He was more like Fallon than himself. Not that he had any of Fallon's guts; I mean his way of speaking was like Fallon's. The words stopped and started.

Dunstan had a belly like a cow in the last month. "Don't drop it in here," I warned him.

The blacksmith wasn't one for words, but he knew how hard his fists were. "Look, you," he said.

"Look at what? At you? I'd rather look at Dunstan."

"Look at me," the blacksmith said, taking a sidelong look at the scared banker.

I shifted the muzzle of the goose-gun so it was staring at the blacksmith. "I don't want to look at you, Horseshoe. You're not pretty enough, like Dunstan."

I began to think the blacksmith might be the only real trouble I was likely to get. That was why they brought him along, I figured. I figured, too, that he was good and drunk. He didn't look drunk when he came in—a man with all that meat to soak up the whiskey can look sober at first—but now I knew he was.

"You better mind your manners, mister," he said

in a rumbling voice. "We come here to talk, not be sassed."

"Talk then," I told Dunstan. "No, Mr. Mayor, I changed my mind. I'll do the talking to save time." Lord, but I was feeling mean. I was mean and getting meaner by the minute because I wanted another drink and the bottle was on the desk and I didn't feel like moving with that drunk and outraged blacksmith to consider.

I'm a great one for changing my mind. That's what happens when you live the way I do. I guess you get used to doing what you Goddamn well like. It's a way of working that just might get me killed some day. I sure hope so. When I finally stop that last bullet I'd hate to have folks say I lived so long because I was too careful.

"You see that bottle of whiskey? You pass it to me. Then you can drink yourself if that's what you want." I was talking to the blacksmith. I didn't mind being polite to the blacksmith. "You can drink, only you," I warned him. "These other gents have had enough."

I watched him with the goose-gun. "Careful, don't spill a drop—it's Old Overshoe."

After bracing Fallon and his two gunslingers I didn't want to get brained by a drunk blacksmith. He didn't try it.

Dunstan and his businessmen friends were waiting. The blacksmith took the bottle back, rammed the cork in with the heel of his hand, then changed his mind, and pulled it out with his teeth.

Whiskey gurgled and Mayor Dunstan made a

face. I swear that sour fat banker was a born reformer: he made so many faces.

"You want me to leave, but I don't want to leave," I said. "That's the start of it. You start off telling me that. Then you ask me why I don't start acting like a nice fella and stop talking tough to Mister Fallon? As a come-back to that, I tell you that Fallon didn't just come here to scatter twenty-dollar bills into the wind. I tell you Fallon came here to fetch back the wife of Big Sam Thornton. None of you gents much less than forty, so you know, you recall, who Big Sam is. That business of burning women and kids down on the Nueces River."

"Never any proof of that," Dunstan protested.

I went on. "Proof or not, you say if I dispute Fallon's story—the hell with that Yankee-loving rancher. That's old business and this is new. Lots of men were in the War and did bad things in the War and after the War. We have some words about that and I say the hell with Sam Thornton. I say, Fallon came here to get Thornton's runaway wife any way he can—like a slave-catcher thirty years ago. I tell you Fallon came here for nothing else. Not to build this miserable town into something better, just to drag Thornton's wife back to Thornton's dirty bed. All right, you argue, that's why he came here, but now that he's here he wants to mix business with the other thing. In case you don't recall the word for that, you miserable sons of storekeepers—that's called pimping."

That didn't bother the blacksmith much, or it

bothered him and he didn't show it. I decided it bothered him, because the bottle gurgled again. Then it bothered him to drink from my bottle, and he set it down on the desk without pushing in the cork.

It bothered Dunstan and the others. I was talking so much I felt like John C. Calhoun getting hoarse over the divine rights of South Carolina.

"We didn't come here to be insulted, Carmody," Dunstan complained, redder in the face than before. It wasn't a good healthy whiskey red in the banker's jowly face. "You have no right . . ."

"You want to talk about it, Dunstan," I said. "All right, I twist the truth and don't call you pimps. You admit that Fallon is a well-paid pimp, but he's also a famous Texas man. Politician, lawyer, businessman—you like that dirty word—and anything else you care to mention. He's doing a favor for a powerful friend and that's all you want to know."

I let that hang for a while.

"You just lost your own argument," Dunstan said. "That's it! You said it: we don't give a damn. This town's dying and we'll grab at anything. The whole of Brewster County is in the middle of hard times. Anything that comes along is worth grabbing for. And you—you're . . . "

"In the way," I said. "Sorry, gents, Mister Mayor and you too, Blacksmith—that's where I stay."

"You won't listen?" the blacksmith asked me.

"Not the way Fallon wants it," I said. "Fallon

71

wants me to sit back and let him bring in gunmen to take the girl. I go fishing, that's what Fallon wants. What you want, I guess."

Dunstan said, "That's not what we want, the businessmen of this town. We want you to get out. The sheriff will be back. It's not your job: let him handle it in his own way."

I said I was sorry not to be able to oblige. "With Luke gone I'm the sheriff."

Sucked in air puffed up Dunstan's wattled face. He made that harrumping noise again. The Mayor was getting set to fire his big gun at me. I got ready for the shock.

"Judge Flanders, if you will," the mayor called out.

I wanted to see Judge Flanders. Luke hadn't said anything about a court in Salter City. Though Luke bent the law and made his nest there, Salter City wasn't the county seat.

I had figured the man with the beaver hat and white whiskers to be the oldest of the assembled storekeepers, maybe the richest or the poorest of the money-grubbers. He gave a jump when he heard his name called; then he dropped a heavy book.

Dunstan was impatient, and I knew I was right about how he divided rich men and poor men. When the so-called judge got under the hanging lamp I saw how poor he was, and how scared. I didn't feel even a gnat's eye worth of pity for the shabby old son of a bitch who was trying to bend his knees enough to pick up the dropped book. The poor old snuffling bastard groping for the book was Dunstan's version of the man-destroying monster gun I held across my knee.

One of the storekeepers got the book for Judge Flanders. Notice how much respect I have for the law and the old men who twist it to suit other men. Notice that I call him Judge Flanders without asking to have the fact of his judgeship proved to me.

"No hurry, your honor," I said kindly.

His honor hadn't been spoken to like that for some time. Every godawful town in Texas, in other states and territories, has a judge like Judge Flanders. A judge like that is like the sway-backed nag nobody wants to buy. They shove a fistful of ginger up his glory hole and trot him out when everything else fails.

"Thank you, Sheriff Carmody," the judge told me, nodding his head in my direction. The trouble was, he couldn't stop nodding once he started. I guess he needed another drink; so did I.

Mayor Dunstan was puffed up like a rooster about to make a surprise attack. If there had been henshit to scratch in, he would have scratched. It was a wonder that he didn't crow. My thought was that he was saving that for later. I hoped the mayor of Salter City wouldn't be too disappointed.

The judge couldn't find his page, and they had to help him again. I guess I never did see a group of citizens more anxious to get the Laws of Texas read out loud.

Judge Flanders found it easier to see once he finally discovered his spectacles. One side was cracked and both sides were dirty; it was better than being blind.

Blinking at me, shaking the law book in shaky hands, he told me I wasn't any kind of lawful sheriff. With his dirty glasses on, the mildewed book in his hands, he steadied up like a gunfighter handed back his gun. Or a drunk with a new full bottle.

"Damn right," the blacksmith agreed.

Judge Flanders had his moment. "Don't interrupt, Mr. Bullock," he said. "Or else . . . or else . . ."

He read me page such and such, paragraph something or other. "No sheriff in any county in the State of Texas shall appoint a substitute, or acting, sheriff without the knowledge, or consent, of the Governor of Texas."

Judge Flanders removed his glasses, closed his law book, and looked at my bottle before he looked at me. He tittered so hard he had to wipe his mouth. He was able to do that by himself. "That's the law, Mr. Carmody, as stated in the Revised Statutes of the State of Texas." Judge Flanders had done his part. Now he darted a quick glance at the men who were holding a bottle, or something, to his head. They didn't say anything. Maybe they wanted more for their bottle.

"That means you're not the sheriff," the judge said. "The sheriff didn't follow the law, so you're not the sheriff. What I mean, Mr. Carmody, you're holding office illegally."

74

I grinned at the judge, thanking him for setting me straight on that troublesome point of law. "I was worried," I said. "You read that good, Judge —just like a real judge."

By the time Judge Flanders figured that out, Mayor Dunstan repeated what the old man had said. "You're finished," he advised me. "Read it yourself if you want to. The law is clear. Do you hear?"

What I said about the clearness of the law was dirty. The wound that troubled me most was getting better, but I was tired, and wanted to kill the rest of Fallon's bottle in peace.

"You heard the law," Dunstan said, surprised at the way I was taking his legal buckshot. "You don't have anything to say? You're not the legal sheriff of Brewster County. You can be arrested and prosecuted for—what is it, Judge?"

Judge Flanders had it on the tip of his tongue, but it slipped off. "For a lot of things," he said.

"That's right," Dunstan · said. "That's what could happen to you. However"—the Mayor tried hard to be a good fella—"there's no need for that. It's clear that the sheriff is to blame. The fact is, we're prepared to pay whatever the sheriff agreed to pay you. Within reason, that is. How much is that?"

"A thousand dollars for three weeks," I said.

Dunstan gulped and his greedy nature fought against saying yes. But he said it, and he didn't call me a liar, which I was.

"What do you say, gentlemen?" he asked the onlooking storekeepers. He didn't wait for an answer. "A thousand it is," he said. "On condition that you get out of town. Now we can't be fairer than that. Come on, man—what do you say?"

I told them to scat.

CHAPTER EIGHT

It got quiet in the jail. I didn't bring up the goose-gun, but I moved it a little. Small though the shift on the gun was, it frightened them. Dunstan was too scared to move; the storekeepers crowded back into the doorway like panicky sheep all trying to get through the same gap.

Dunstan was ready to run if the others would give him room; if I didn't kill him while he ran. Judge Flanders, so-called, wasn't afraid of the goose-gun. Neither was the blacksmith named Bullock. They had different reasons for not being scared: the judge was sick of life and more afraid of being poor than being dead, and the blacksmith was too big and too drunk to care.

I expected fists from the blacksmith—not talk. The judge had said his piece, read his bullshit laws; it hadn't worked too well. The blacksmith moved out in front of the others. I told him to move back. I said my party was over. "Fallon's shindig is still going," I said. "Go back there."

Only a brave or a very stupid man would have talked back to a man with a sawed-off goose-gun in his hands. The blacksmith was both, and it came to the same thing.

There was a problem about how to handle him. I had to stop him if he kept coming. Sure I could blow him out through the door with a light squeeze of the trigger. When the smoke cleared, the blacksmith, the mayor and most of the leading citizens of Salter City would be nothing but a pile of stewing meat. And that wasn't really the idea.

Now the blacksmith was telling me I had no right to stand in the way of the town's good fortune. I guess the poor lumbering fool really believed that better days were on their way. "You got no right," he said. "I got kids, mister, and I can't hardly feed them. I'm not asking you to stand aside."

I stood up holding the gun. "Move on out," I warned the big man. "All you gents move. You want me to make a count?"

They turned suddenly and ran, and it was a good thing there were no women and kids, because they'd have been trampled. The blacksmith stayed where he was. "You too, Horseshoe," I said.

"You wouldn't talk so tough without that gun," he growled, swaying on his feet, smelling of whiskey and sweat.

"Course not," I said. "That's why I got this gun, so I can talk tough. Now you get."

"No, I won't do that," he answered, shaking his thick head. "You're the one in the wrong. You're the one is leaving."

I was tired of talk. I didn't want to hear any more about his hungry kids. And it wasn't because of his hungry kids that I didn't blow off both his legs at the knee. He was close enough to get hit in the belly with the muzzle of the gun. The barrel dug in hard but it didn't knock the wind out of him. I upended the heavy weapon and tried to cave in his face with the stock. I didn't get to do it, and maybe the gun was too heavy for such a quick move. He clamped both hands on the gun, quick as a cat for a big man, and would have tossed me and the gun across the room if I hadn't let go.

My gunbelt was hung over the back of the chair. I twisted out of his way and was grabbing for my handgun when he hit me a mulekick of a punch in the back of the head. Another man would have wrecked his hand; that blacksmith had hands like seasoned wood. He kicked me behind the knee while I was still falling. All I could think of was the gunbelt. White lights were flashing in my head. I could see the gunbelt. My hands were clawing for it, but instead of kicking me the blacksmith moved around me fast and kicked the chair out of the way. Figuring he'd wade in again with more kicks I rolled away from him. That gave my head a few seconds to start thinking again. The blacksmith moved fast, but not at me. He scooped up belt and gun and slung them out through the door. "We'll see how tough . . ." he was saying. He grabbed the empty bottle and broke it on the wall.

The son of a bitch turned his back on me and went after the goose-gun. I took a flying leap and tackled him from behind. My arms got him around the middle; it was like trying to bring down a tree. He kept moving, dragging me behind him. I hooked a heel in front of his ankle, and we both staggered and fell. Bear-hugging him wasn't worth trying. Like I said, it was like trying to break a tree in the middle. The worst of it was, there was nothing to hit him with but my fists. We rolled on the floor. I tried to use the knee on him, and that didn't work either. He was up before I was. He let me get up most of the way, grinning at me. I lowered my head and went at his belly like a mad bull. I should have remembered that his belly was as hard as his hands. It was like using your head to batter down a barn door. My head hurt. It hurt worse when his big paws clamped on both sides of it. I expected a knee in the face, but that wasn't what he did. What he did was try to twist my head off my shoulders. Then, I swear, he used my head to lift me off the floor. I don't know how big that big bastard was, a good six inches taller than me, a hundred pounds heavier. Even so, he had to use all his heat-forged muscles to throw me at the back wall of the jail. He managed to do it. My back hit the wall and I sat down hard.

He bent down and came up with the goose-gun in his hands. In his hands the big gun looked small. He was laughing now, having a good time, and it wasn't because he thought I was keeping food from his starving kids. He cocked the gun and held it in one hand, his thick finger curled around the trigger, grinning like a wild man. I don't know what I thought when I saw that monster gun cocked and aimed at me.

Just for a second or two, there wasn't a sound. Just the two of us standing there with the God-damned music drifting over from the hotel. One thing I can't stomach is a man about to kill me with a grin on his face. I called him a dirty name to hurry it up.

"You're scared sick," he sneered. "You and your stinking guns . . ."

He set down the hammer and tossed the sawed-off into the street. I guess I blinked at that. How often do you look into the gaping muzzle of a sawed-off and get another chance?

Balling his fists he moved in slowly, running off at the mouth as he did. "Here's where you get taught a lesson," he said. "First I'm going to beat you till your guts come loose. Then I'm going to kick the lungs clear out of your chest. Then I'm going to stomp on your hands till they're jam. You ain't never going to use another gun in your life. Here or no place else."

The only thing I could see to use on him was the broken chair. There was a leg with part of a rung stuck to it. He didn't even try to keep me from grabbing it. He moved in easily, grinning all the time, fists balled hard and held shoulder high. I swung at his face and he blocked it with his forearm. If it hurt he didn't show it. He didn't even try to take the chair leg away from me, not at first. The next time I feinted with the piece of wood. He moved his arm to block it and I hit him along the side of the head. His ear puffed up as soon as the blow landed, but the wild grin on his face didn't change.

He took another whack across the side of the neck. It was like hitting a side of beef for all the good it did me. "Lesson time," he said. I swung the chair leg again. It smacked against his open hand, then his huge hand snapped shut like a steel trap. I hung onto the chair leg and he knocked me loose with a punch delivered with his other hand. Then he deadened my right arm with the chair leg before he threw it away.

"Now!" he grunted.

I went at him again using every dirty trick I ever learned. I know a lot of dirty tricks and one or two should have worked. He grunted a bit when I tried to kick off his kneecap with the toe of my boot. That was all he did—he grunted. There was that much meat and muscle on the big bastard, and all of it was hard. He crowded me against the back wall again making no effort to block the punches I threw at his grinning, meaty face.

When I couldn't back off any more, he started body punching. The stink of sweat and whiskey was strong in my face. I felt the trickle of blood and knew the wound in my side had broken open. That made me mad because that Goddamned hole had taken so long to heal. It didn't do me much good to get mad. Nothing I was doing was much good.

He hit me again, then grabbed my shirt and pulled me away from the wall. Jesus, I don't mind being punched, but I hate being open-handed. That's what he did. With my shirt bunched in his hand he slapped me with the other hand. The shirt tore loose and I went flying back against the desk. He jumped after me, trying to throw me on top of the desk. Papers rustled under my hand and I remembered the desk spike where Luke stuck the reward posters. I grabbed the heavy metal base of the spike and shook it loose from the stack of papers. I don't think he saw the spike. If he did it was too late. He rushed in on me and I shoved the needle-pointed spike through his chest. I was trying for the heart and got him through the right lung. That's what it looked like—the right lung.

It went in smooth as a hot knife through butter. Not a bone got in the way to turn back the long thin bar of steel. With all that whiskey in him, he didn't feel it right away. Maybe he didn't even know it was there. I rolled over the desk and landed on my feet. He roared and grabbed the desk with both hands and began to lift it. That was the first and only time any man tried to throw a desk at me. He almost made it. He got it chest high in one powerful pull like a weight lifter. There was some blood on the front of his white shirt; not much.

The grin was still on his face. He tried to keep it there. Then he looked surprised as the strength drained from his arms. The desk wavered and crashed to the floor. His hand came up and touched the base of the spike. He held out his hand and looked at the blood. Putting one foot in front of the other like a man walking in deep snow, he tried to come after me. I was too tired to hit the son of a bitch. I moved out of his way and waited till he fell. That's what it was like—a tree falling.

He lay on his back, the spike in his chest, his eyes open. Words came from his mouth, but I didn't understand them.

"Shut up and lie still," I told him. "Maybe you'll die and maybe you won't.

I figured Dunstan and his friends hadn't gone far. They were out in the dark and they tried to sneak away when I went to pick up the guns from the street. Before I went outside I found the key and unchained my Winchester. I should have worried that the goose-gun had gotten into the wrong hands, but it was still lying where the blacksmith had thrown it. Dunstan was leading his pack of rats back to the hotel as fast as they could drag their fat bellies. Out of pure meanness, I thought of letting off the goose-gun. It was a good idea, but I didn't do it.

Word of the fight, if you can call it that, had

gone out. The two boys from the livery stable came to gawk. I waved them away from the door and told them to hunt up some kind of doctor. "Hurry it up," I said.

Finley, the talky one clapped his hand to the side of his head. "Holy Moley!" he said. "Did you beat up Mr. Bullock that way?"

His brother Todd said, "Town doesn't have a doctor, if you don't count Mr. Frimmell who sets bones."

"Go get him," I said. "Don't weasel me for money, you little bastard—go fetch him."

The two kids ran off yelling about the big fight, and I told the gawkers to get the hell home. I was doing that when Fallon and his two gunmen came out of the hotel and stood looking at the jail. Then Dunstan and some of the storekeepers came out too. Dunstan was talking and Fallon was nodding his head. Judge Flanders was there, but he wasn't too interested. He had a bottle in his hand.

I went back inside and closed the door but didn't bar it. The blacksmith lay there like a wounded grizzly. His beefy red face had turned white in patches; the skin that hadn't turned white was redder than before. His eyes were open and staring at the ceiling, and when he took in air the wound in his chest made a bubbling sound. There was still very little blood on his shirt; that didn't mean he wasn't leaking fast inside. He croaked for water, and I didn't give it to him.

"No water now—don't talk," I said.

I didn't especially want him to die and I wasn't

praying for him to get well. It would make my general problem a little bit worse if he died—but not much. The fact was, it was getting worse every minute I let Fallon run loose.

The stable boys were coming back with the bonesetter. I didn't want them in there gaping at the wounded man, but I figured the bonesetter might need some help. When they got inside I told them to bar the door.

The bonesetter was a frail old gent with a dry papery face. Straightening out busted bones takes some strength; this old gent didn't look like he had it. He walked over to the blacksmith and looked at him like a vet looking at an injured horse.

He snuffled for a while before he spoke. "Worse than a broken leg, I reckon."

"Skip the talk," I said. "Can you help him or do we let him die in peace?"

"Not for you to say, maybe not for me to say. He dies in peace or torment—that's his business. There isn't a thing I can do—nor the best doctor going—but pull that thing out of his chest, cover the wound, and make him rest. You do this, did you? Must have had a good reason. I always did say Mr. Bullock would meet a bigger man some day."

I didn't feel like laughing at the bonesetter's joke. "Do anything you want with him. If you can't fix him—then bury him. If he lives he's under arrest for attempted murder. Don't worry, you'll be paid. Just bill the county. Doctor him the best you can, but don't do it here."

After they took away the blacksmith in a wagon bed softened with hay, I barred the door and turned down the lamp. Luke had only one chair and that was broken. The bottle was broken and I felt pretty busted-up myself. The pink-white hole in my side had stopped bleeding; now it was caked shut with dried blood. And I'll say it again: I hurt like a son of a bitch.

Not much else was definite.

CHAPTER NINE

In the morning, the kid called Finley came around to tell me it looked like the blacksmith might live. That was the good—or bad—news from the old man who had doctored him.

I was back from breakfast, and by now even the old fry-cook didn't have much to say to me. I guess he was thinking of his business, such as it was.

I'd been thinking about Finley. He was too young to consider that hanging around the jail could make him unpopular with his boss and the rest of the town.

"Todd wants to be a businessman, a big one," he informed me. "Not me."

"That a fact," I said.

It was hot as hell even so early in the morning, but I couldn't be up and down the street every time I wanted coffee, so I had a fire going in Luke's potbelly and a pot of coffee made and set back to simmer blacker than it was.

"That's right," Finley said.

"You'd as soon be a lawman, is that it?" I asked him.

"Nothing else," he answered. "Todd can have his ledgers and account books. The hell with that, Mr. Carmody. There's more money in it—I know that—but where's the glory, I want to know?"

Luke's office was as shabby as the salvation room of a city mission; as battered as a Mexican camp follower.

"Not here," I said.

Finley didn't mind that. "Maybe not here," he said. "I admit that. But that's what I'd like to be—a lawman. Don't try to talk me out of it."

I still can't remember what Finley looked like. "Wouldn't think of it," I said. "You want to start right now?"

"You mean it?"

"Maybe. You know what's going on in Salter City?"

"Sure," the boy said.

I asked him to explain.

"You got most of it," I said. "Some of it anyhow. You know you could get killed helping me?"

Finley had a question. "I'd get paid, wouldn't I?"

That was the idea, I said, not wanting to make use of the kid, but there was nobody else in Salter City I could even think about trusting.

"Then it's all right," he decided. "Doesn't have to be much. Isn't the money, I mean. But if I didn't get paid I wouldn't feel like I was doing any good. Mr. Carmody, what do I have to do?" Finley made his face look serious. "Before my daddy died he taught me to shoot. That was a time ago. Maybe I could work at it."

"No guns," I said. "You ride north to the telegraph wires and send a message. That's what you're to do—nothing but."

Disappointment clouded his face. He had a fair command of bad language, for a boy. "That ain't nothing, Mr. Carmody," he said. "Ain't you got nobody else for that?"

"Don't be like that, boy." I went over it again.

"I'll do it," he said. "Want me to go now?"

I said when it got dark; if not then—when it was safe to go without being spotted. "They could be watching the road," I said. "You sure you want to do this? Maybe Brother Todd has it right. You think rubbing down horses is nothing. It's some better than laying dead in the dust."

The kid asked if he could have a cup of coffee, explaining that he was purely sick of buttermilk. Buttermilk wasn't my drink either. I penciled the message on the back of a wanted poster and gave it to him.

A slow reader, Finley got as far as To Governor, State of Texas before he whistled long and loud.

"Depend on me, Mr. Carmody." He paused. "Woud two dollars be asking too much? They say deputies get that much."

"Do it right and you'll get a month's pay—sixty," I said.

Coffee spilled out of his cup. "Lord, wait'll I tell Todd."

"Don't," I said. "You figure it."

Most of the fifty Luke gave me was left, about forty dollars. I gave him twenty. "Get out of here, boy, you been in here too long—and thanks!"

It was still early, still quiet—but not for long. I was working on the rest of the coffee when I heard yelling down the street. The yelling started and stopped. The sound of boots clopping in the dust followed the yelling. My first thought was that Fallon's man had come back with the rest of his bravos.

I was wrong. The noise came from the south end of town and Fallon's men wouldn't be coming in from that direction, not without a good reason. To do that they'd have to ride around. I went outside and blinked some in the hard sun.

It wasn't just the sun. No, sir. What I blinked at was Zack Eldredge riding into town on about the oldest horse I ever saw. A man like that would ride a nag like that. Allowing for the difference in the ages of men and horses, Zack's cayuse was older than he was. It was a white horse gone gray with hard use. It sagged in the middle and its ribs stuck out. Probably it could manage a downhill trot, but nothing could make it gallop.

Zack and his nag were out in front. Some of the other Eldredge men had mounts, a few horses, the rest mules. Hardly an animal there that hadn't seen better days. Zack's boys rode in close to a buckboard that had Sally Eldredge, and the boy, Willy, holding the reins. Just one woman and all those wild men with rifles.

Sally didn't look any too happy. There were about as many Eldredges there as I'd seen out at their place; and they rode—and walked—into Salter City as cocky as Sherman's looters must have been when they reached the sea.

It was what the military gents call a show of strength. The town was surprised, and so was I. All they needed to make it official was a flag. I didn't know what they could put on their flag. A squirrel rifle leaning against the side of a half-mooned outhouse with a coon hound watching it?

One of Fallon's bully boys was carrying a tray of food from the restaurant to the hotel. He didn't drop the tray, but he did hurry up. Then everybody was off the street except me and the Eldredges.

I stood outside the jail and waited. A fool might have laughed at the way they looked; nobody else would have. I knew that every rifle in the bunch had a bullet chambered or primed to let fly.

The town watched from windows and doors. Fallon's hotel room fronted on the street. There was a movement behind the curtains, then it stopped.

I knew as much as the town did. The Eldredges weren't carrying cans of coal oil; that didn't mean they couldn't burn Salter City flat with one match.

They kept coming, taking no heed of the hotel. Old Zack had no saddle, just a folded blanket. Zack stopped in front of me. Civil enough, he nodded to me and I nodded back. I said, "Morning."

"Hot," he said.

"That's true," I agreed.

"Has been hotter," Zack went on.

He didn't have to raise himself to look at the town. Robert E. himself, looking out over Gettysburg, couldn't have done it better.

"Anything I can do for you?" I asked as if we'd never met before.

Zack's fierce old eyes came back to rest on me. "Nobody does nothing for me." My shotgun didn't bother him. "I'm here to say something. I guess you don't know my daughter Sally?"

It was kind of an introduction. I needed both hands to hold the shotgun steady, so I nooded. Sally didn't do anything.

Zack brought his rasping voice up to a full roar. "I hear some folks in town been asking questions about this daughter of mine. You hear that, Sheriff?"

"Something like that," I told him. I wondered how Fallon was feeling along about then.

Zack was roaring again, a South Texas Abraham in dirty overalls. With all that roaring, Fallon's name wasn't spoken once. "Any man wants to ask questions about my girl—now's the time," the old man bellowed, adding that this man, whoever he

94

was, was nothing less than an offal-eating, cross-eyed, yellow-backed son of a mangy bitch.

I thought that was a fair description of Malachi Fallon. Except for the cross-eyed part.

Zack, louder than before, was telling the silent town what they did to men like that back in Georgia. "A town that takes up with a man like that deserves the fire and brimstone . . ."

I didn't care about the brimstone, so I warned the old man about fire. "Not this town," I said, shifting the muzzle of the 8 gauge shotgun. Just a touch on the trigger and Zack and about five of his boys would go flying home to hell. The girl too.

"You figure to stop us with that, do you?" the old man wanted to know, taking notice of the shotgun for the first time. "We ain't geese, mister."

That was for sure: they looked more like a hungry wolfpack. "Gun's been worked on," I said, telling him what he already knew. "Tell the girl to move before you decide."

A glint of hard humor showed in his eyes. "You'd have a better edge if she stayed put."

"Your daughter," I told him. "Now I say you won't burn this town. Least you won't, Zack."

"Not today I won't," Zack announced. "Didn't plan to do it today. If I did the place would be falling over by now." He was off and roaring again. "When we come—if we come—it'll be in the dark. Why, friends and neighbors, we'll make Lawrence, Kansas, look like a church supper. That's the sermon for today, you town-living nest of snakes, and if you're slow getting the point, here it is. No more talking about my daughter, no more taking sides. The next man even speaks my girl's name is going to get killed . . ."

"You going now?" I asked.

"Not just yet. We come and go as we please. Now we please to stay for a while. Drink a few drinks, lay in some provisions. Kind of let the town see us up close. Don't you fret about my boys getting out of line. First one does a wrong thing I'll kill him. He'd be surprised if I didn't."

I told him to keep the killing in the family. "You said your piece, now leave the town be. Fallon knows you mean business."

"Is that his name?" the old man sneered. "Never heard of him. About the town. I'll leave it be just so long. But not because you say so."

He turned and told his boys to drink some whiskey, and they were more than ready to do that. The boy took the buckboard to a hitching post and Sally Eldredge got down.

"That's a good-looking gun," the old man said, nodding his hat brim that way. "What is it—a Davenport?"

"Eight-gauge, thirty-six inch barrel. The barrel's shorter now. They say one blast knocks down a grizzly."

"It won't knock me down," Eldredge said.

CHAPTER TEN

"Come in," I said to the light tap on the side of the open door.

Sally Eldredge walked in wearing a different dress than I'd seen her in out at the farm. It was fancy, and so was she. "Time we had a talk, Carmody."

I thought so myself. More and more I'd been thinking that she ought to leave town. I asked her if she wanted a drink. When she didn't answer I set out bottle and glasses. "This parade your idea?" I asked.

"No," she said. "You don't want to talk about that. Talk about something else."

She didn't want to sit in my new chair. It was the only chair I had. She walked the length of the office; not much of a walk.

"Your turn," she said. "You ask and I'll answer—maybe."

"How'd you get mixed up with Thornton?"

Sally looked at me like I wasn't overburdened with brains. "How'd you think. I was just a kid when we left Georgia. It was bad there and worse in Texas, if that's possible. You saw what it looks like. I still got some brothers who don't see me as different from any other woman. I can handle them now, but I couldn't then. Anyway, that was just part of it. Anyway, I lit out when I was sixteen. Daddy chased me for a bit, then gave up."

"Daddy's not as determined as Thornton," I suggested.

Sally flared up at that. "Don't you start dumping on my father," she said. "Even if I do hate the son of a bitch."

"No harm meant," I said. "Go on."

"The old story," she said. "This and that. Clerking in a store, waitressing in dirty restaurants, making beds in a hotel, stuffing pillows in a factory. Those were some of the good jobs I worked at. You'd think a girl like me could do better than I did, but I couldn't. There was always some wet-handed bastard trying to lift my skirts for free. Men, with all their brag, are such lousy cheapskates. I did the whole tour, all the big dirty towns. There were a lot of men and never much money. Then I got a job dealing cards in Mossy Jennings gambling place in New Orleans. Then I got Mossy himself—I was glad to grab that fat old man."

She paused and I kept quiet.

Sally put a tough look on her face. "I didn't like Mossy and I didn't hate him too much. He was old and easy to handle. About once a month was Mossy's speed. It might have worked out if Thornton hadn't come around to ask Mossy why he was taking so long to make up his mind about coming in with him. Thornton was putting the boots to every gambler and brothel-keeper in New Orleans. I was there when Thornton came to call with three of his top gunmen. He kept looking at me. Mossy decided in a hurry, but that wasn't enough for Thornton. Mossy got his back up about that and said the deal was off. That night he went out and never came back. Nobody ever saw him again. That same night Thornton's men came to get me . . ."

That could be the way it happened; there might have been a fat old man who couldn't go faster than once a month. Or, knowing something about women like Sally, it could be just one more hard-luck story. "You didn't argue and here you are," I said.

"Nobody argues with Sam Thornton," she said. "Besides, Mossy was dead and I was alive."

I said that was a sensible way to look at it. I didn't mean it as a slap in the face. "If you were so sensible about it, what caused the trouble?"

"Not me," she said. "I didn't ask Thornton to take me to his fancy house. A room in a fair hotel would have suited me better. I didn't ask him to marry me, but that's what he said he wanted. All right, I was ready to keep my part of the bargain. I had a big house with servants, and what happened in bed wasn't that important to me, not after the way I lived. But Thornton, being a lot older than me and not much good to any woman, didn't want to believe I was on the level. Couldn't believe I wasn't always looking to sneak off with some man. One minute he was mushing all over me, the next throwing me down the stairs."

I knew that part was true; Sam Thornton was known to have a way with women. I let her go on.

"Jesus, it was pure hell not knowing what to expect. He'd start asking questions about Mossy Jennings, about other men. No matter what I said, I was a liar and an ignorant no-good Georgia cracker slut. I don't know why a dirty East Texas pig farmer would want to call me that. Then he'd say he was sorry and start slobbering all over me again. He kept giving parties all the time for his politician friends—the ones on his payroll—but if any man less than sixty danced with me he'd get killing mad. One night he got so drinking mad he shot one of the colored men in the orchestra. Now why in hell did he have to do that?"

"Less trouble than shooting a state senator," I said. "What else?"

"What else is there? He didn't get worse. He was worse when he started. I thought I could stand it long enough to get some money together before I made a break. I never did manage to get very much. Thornton watched me all the time and when he wasn't watching me somebody else was."

I finished rolling a cigarette and put it in my mouth. "So you didn't get any money out of all that grief," I said. "You cut and ran empty-handed?"

"Less than a hundred dollars. I'd call that empty-handed."

"Pretty much," I agreed. "Seems a shame you didn't get something out of it. No argument about Sam Thornton—he's an animal." I put a match to the tobacco, looking at her through the first curl of smoke. "You know about the woman and kids he burned when you married him?"

I expected her to say no. Most women would have said no. This one didn't. Maybe she wanted to say no, but figured I wouldn't believe her. "I knew something about it," she told me. "It's still talked of in New Orleans, not out loud though. The truth is, I didn't give a damn. That was Thornton's business. My business was me."

"And here you are," I said again. "The question is—do you stay?"

Instead of answering she asked me to fix her a smoke. "Never could roll one," she said.

I said yep.

"Here I stay," she said. "I been everywhere else since I ran off."

I gave her the cigarette and lit it for her. "He found you here," I said. "Where's the difference?" It wasn't very gentlemanly, trying to edge her out of town that way, but it was one way to get rid of the trouble.

What I'd said made her smile. "Maybe finding me won't do him any good. I'm safer here than with the whole New York police force guarding me. A lot safer, the way bluecoats take money. I got me a lot of kinfolk, and from Cousin Willy to Daddy Zack there isn't man nor boy can't break a thrown bottle with the first shot. You yourself didn't get far."

It was funny to hear her bragging about her dirty dangerous clan. I knew how well they could shoot, and how ready to do it. I knew Fallon, if left to himself, would shy away from them. So would I.

"You got a good family to stay away from," I said. "I'd say that because I'm a man with some sense. How much sense does Sam Thornton have?"

"Not much when he gets mad," she admitted. That made her think of something. "I guess you don't know the real reason he killed that farmer's family?"

The killing down on the Nueces River had happened a long time ago. Before he started telling people he didn't do it at all, Thornton used to yarn about how the dead farmer had been a Yank guerilla in the War; how this Confederate-hating farmer tried to bushwhack him and his men, all good veterans of Hood's army, when they rode in like lambs to beg for provisions. Thornton used to say he didn't know the woman and kids were in that barn when he burned it. In self defense, naturally.

102

That's what I repeated to Sally.

Her laugh had iron filings in it. "Thornton burned them because they had no whiskey on the place. They were temperance people, Quakers—something like that. That's the plain truth of it. No whiskey when Sam was thirsty, so he killed a whole family. You know how I know? He told me himself."

She was trying to get me on her side. I believed what she said, but I wasn't going against Sam Thornton because of something that had happened a long time before on the Nueces River. I didn't like her to try to get at me that way. She was the one who had married the child-killer.

"Sam always did like a drink," I said. "And that answers the question about his good sense."

The story about the farmer had turned the argument against her, but she kept at it. "Then you don't think Thornton will give up when Fallon sends back word how hard it is to take me?"

I was thinking about another kind of taking. Looking at her, listening to the rustle of her silk dress, the smell of her perfume, I didn't blame Sam Thornton one bit. I would never send a bunch of hired guns to fetch any woman, but for this one I'd do some hard riding on my own.

I said, "My guess—Fallon doesn't have to send back word. I think Fallon has his orders—bring you back, or something happens to Fallon. You don't happen to know what Thornton is holding over Fallon to make him work so hard?"

She didn't know exactly—but something impor-

103

tant. Then she told me what I'd figured already; that Thornton had picked Fallon because he thought Fallon could do it the easy way, the quiet way, keep his name out of it, buy off or scare off the local law, use his political pull to wet-blanket any future trouble.

"Thornton's still hoping to buy a pardon," she told me. "That's why he doesn't want any trouble in Texas. Otherwise..."

I finished it for her.

She had a thought—not a new thought. "You're the local law, Carmody. Not even the steady law. Why aren't you bought off? Your rich daddy sending you money?"

"All I got is a cousin and he's the sheriff," I said. "You know that. What you don't know is he'll sell you down the river if this thing drags on till he gets back. Much as I hate to say it—that's Cousin Luke."

"And you won't try to stop him?"

"Not my own kin. You ought to understand that, having such a family feeling as you do. Besides, I wouldn't be sheriff any longer." I tapped my chest. "Off the payroll and out from behind this badge. Out of town too since Luke won't be begging me to stay. We're cousins, but we're not real close."

She moved in close to me. I liked how she smelled: perfume and soap. All that traveling around had taught her things. From a wild mountain girl she had come fairly close to looking and sounding like a lady. She ran her hands across my face like an old blind lady checking out her long lost son.

"Then you can't be bought," she suggested.

I grinned at her. "Now that is a fool thing to say. I'm always ready to be bought for a good cause. Even a not so good cause. Just not as dirty as Fallon's."

It was nice having her plastered up against me. Nice, too, having her kiss me like her life depended on it, which in a way it did.

"I'm glad you feel that way," she said. "Good to meet a real man for a change. I think you better put the bar on the door."

I thought that was a right smart idea. I didn't know what I'd do if Daddy Zack came a-calling, but you learn not to get ahead of yourself.

"I'll be good to you," she murmured, leading me into Luke's iron-barred bedroom. And so she was, going at it a mite faster than is usual, but not so hasty that anything was wasted. I wondered what crazy Sam Thornton would do when he heard, if Fallon had enough nerve to tell him, that his wandering wife had spent the best part of an hour inside a locked jail with a lanky galoot named Carmody. Maybe this time he'd slaughter a whole band of musicians.

Already we were like an old married couple. "Do me up," she told me, getting back into her dress.

I was a bit fumble-fingered, but I managed to button her up. She turned around and said, "Well?" as if she expected me to sign a contract, or make some sort of binding statement.

105

I didn't know what to say. "Fine" was all I could think to say.

Impatience broke through at last. "Never mind that," she said quickly. "Will you help me?"

"About the money," I started.

She got it in about two seconds, but she went back to playing wide-eyed. "I don't understand. If you mean do I have any money—I don't. I told you that. Was that what you meant?"

I nodded.

"Don't you believe me?"

"Afraid not. Hate to talk money at a time like this, but might as well. I figure you feathered your nest before you left New Orleans. Yeh, I know what you said—Thornton spying on you night and day—but you're a smart girl. You'd figure a way. Now's the time to spread it around. Nothin cements a friendship like money, I always say."

Spots of red burned in her face and her voice shook with anger. She did it well, but I knew this girl was tough as boardinghouse steak. "You're worse than Fallon," she said. "No, wait a minute. I'm sorry I said that. I know what it's like to want money."

Some women move around when they tell big lies, when they start giving a performance for a man. The tough ones, the real smart ones, can sit still and lie to your face. Sally wasn't that tough yet. She walked up and down smacking one hand against the other. She even managed to squeeze out a few tears.

I was busy buttoning my pants.

Stopping, she chided me with, "I thought you'd be different."

I pulled on my boots and buckled the gunbelt. "Why is that—do I look different? I thought I looked about average greedy."

Ignoring that, she said with a sad, fake smile: "I'm in bad trouble and I know it. Don't you think I'd offer you money if I had any?"

"Maybe not," I said.

"You don't have to sneer at me, Carmody. If you want money bad enough to step on a woman you should have listened to Fallon."

She was fighting hard to keep her temper from running wild. She repeated what she'd said about Fallon. I guess that was supposed to make me feel just awful, something lower than a crawling snake.

"You could be right," I agreed. "Maybe I should listen."

Her temper came out suddenly like the bull in a Juarez bullring. I moved the bottle and glasses so she wouldn't have anything to throw, if it came to that. She wasn't as strong as the blacksmith; she couldn't throw the desk. I smiled at her.

She was still looking for something to throw. When she stopped that she asked how much. "I asked you a question, you no-good bastard. How much?"

"I don't know," I said. "How much do you have?"

She said that was her business and her money. I suppose I had taken what they call unfair advantage of her, letting her seduce me that way, letting

107

her believe a fine upstanding acting sheriff like me could be bribed by a roll in the hay. But, truth to tell, I didn't feel like any kind of snake or barn rat. Truth to tell, I felt fine.

"What about a hundred dollars?" she asked next.

I said what about it.

She told me not to act dumb. "That's the limit," she said. "All I can afford and . . ."

"I know," I said. "And you can't afford that. Tell you what, I won't be greedy. Cousin Luke's paying me five hundred to watch the store. Match that and I'll watch you too. This offer will not be repeated more than ten times. Save time, honey— say yes."

She pretended to give it some thought. "You're a son of a bitch, mister, but all right."

Twisting her face spitefully, she warned me not to expect any more of what she'd given me back in the cells. "I won't pay two ways."

"You will if I say so," I told her.

"You're a fine sheriff, you know that?"

"The finest there is. I'll tell you how fine I am. If we both come out of this and you try a double-cross, I'll rope you and deliver you to Thornton in person. Just wanted you to know how fine I can be."

"You'll get your dirty money," she said.

"I'll trust you," I said. "Now why don't you collect your kinfolk and get out of here?"

She flounced out the door and I never saw a madder female, nor a better-looking one.

Sitting around, waiting for the first Eldredge to go whiskey-mad, I was surprised when not a damn thing happened. It was like seeing a wild bunch of Texas trailherders push cows through heat and cold, mud and dust, all the way to Kansas, and then do nothing but sit around like good little boys.

I was as glad as the rest of the town to see them pack up their goods and leave.

CHAPTER ELEVEN

I didn't expect to see Finley back so soon. It was early afternoon the next day, and three men with Texas Ranger circled-stars brought him into town roped across the back of a horse. The blacksmith had died during the night, and I was something more unpopular than a smallpox epidemic. I didn't care about the Goddamned blacksmith, but I felt bad about the kid.

I'd got into the habit of walking around with that shotgun in my hand. The three Rangers got down and hitched their animals while I watched, and you could almost hear the buzz that went through the town. I saw Dunstan with his head stuck out the door of the bank.

Two of the Rangers were young; the man in charge was in his early forties. He had a long brown face seamed by years of sun, and a close-clipped mustache with gray in it. "I'm Captain Dallgrin." He jerked the thumb of his left hand. "Rangers Clum and Bagley." The other men gave stiff nods. "We got a dead boy here. You know him?"

The mayor was coming up the street followed by some of his friends. Fallon's two gunmen came out of the hotel and stood on the porch, but there was no sign of Fallon.

"Boy's name is Finley. Don't know the last name. Used to work at the livery stable. How'd you happen to find him?"

Dunstan had arrived and was shaking his finger at me. "I'm charging that man with murder," the banker said in a high voice. "He's no sheriff and never was a sheriff. He's holding office illegally and by force and he just murdered one of your finest citizens. I'm telling you to arrest him."

The Ranger Captain spoke to the mayor without taking his eyes off me. "Hold your tongue, mister. I don't take orders from nobody but the State of Texas. You, Sheriff, you don't need that shotgun. I'm taking over here till this thing is straightened out."

I held onto the shotgun. "What thing?"

He took a folded paper from his shirt pocket and

112

slapped it open. Again he used his left hand. He held it out. "You give this to the boy?"

"Looks like it," I said. "You were just riding along and stumbled over a dead boy with a paper in his pocket, is that it?"

Dallgrin narrowed his eyes and his voice got tough. "I don't answer questions, mister, I ask them. I'm here because the Governor sent me to see what was going on down this way. You got any arguments, take them up with the Governor."

Dallgrin was beginning to lose his patience with me. "One more time I'm going to tell you, mister. I'm the law here now. Down that shotgun and shuck that badge. You don't do one thing more till I send in a report and get an answer."

"Now you're talking," Mayor Dunstan chimed in. "Don't take any chances, put the irons on him."

"Button up," Dallgrin rasped. "You're making it worse," he said to me.

"Sure thing—Kessler!"

They all went for their guns at one time. Kessler was faster than the others, but they were all good boys. Not one of them got off a shot though, or if they did I didn't hear it. The 8-gauger boomed once in my hands and the three riders turned into meat. Kessler was closer than the others and he took the main charge. There was plenty of lead left over for the others. It didn't just knock them off their feet while it killed them. It sent them rolling and kept them rolling. I went rolling too as Fallon's two gunmen got over their surprise and opened up from the hotel porch. Bullets whanged off the brick wall of the jail as I hit the dirt, breaking open the shotgun at the same time. The mayor and his friends were crawling and staggering around in sheer panic. A bullet scattered dust in my face as I rolled again. I thumbed a fat heavy cartridge into the shotgun and snapped it shut. The rolling took me into the middle of the street with bullets chasing me. I guess they didn't want to face that shotgun, because suddenly they stopped shooting and bolted for the hotel door. They would have made it if they hadn't tried to get through at the same time.

I stood up and blew them through the closed door. They went into the lobby in a shower of glass and wood splinters. I loaded another cartridge on the run; this one was for Fallon. I just hoped he'd make me use it, and maybe I'd use it no matter what he did. One of the dead men inside the door had no head, the other was shy an arm. I went up the stairs quick and easy, still wanting to square things for the dead boy. I expected Fallon's door to be closed and locked; instead it was open.

"Fallon!" I roared. "I got something for you!"

I couldn't see him. He yelled back that he had no gun. "No gun, you hear that? You can't kill me, I got no gun. You want me alive, Carmody. I got information you want. You hear me?"

I still wanted to kill him, but what he said made sense. I had to tell myself that more than once before I was ready to believe it. Some of the tension drained away and I told him to show himself.

"You mean it?" he yelled back.

"Now, Fallon," I called out. "Right now!"

He came out with his hands raised, sweat beading his rubbery face, and I didn't do a thing until he reached the stairs with the gun in his back. I told him to hold still while I slapped him down for a hidden gun. I ripped off his shirt and pushed him down the stairs. He was down on his hands and knees yelling about a twisted ankle and I kicked him squarely in the kidneys. That started him screaming.

"Up and out," I said. "That's just the beginning."

I shoved him out into the street and the scared faces that looked from doors and windows were like faces caught by a camera when they didn't expect it. The mayor wasn't to be seen; I yelled for him to come out. It was time the mayor learned a few facts about his friend Malachi.

"Come out, Dunstan," I roared. "Come out or I'll come after you."

Dunstan came out of the bank like a man going to face the hangman. "Follow along, Mr. Mayor," I ordered him. "Mr. Fallon has things to tell us, don't you, Mr. Fallon?"

I scratched the back of Fallon's neck with the muzzle of the shotgun. "Just don't kill me," he pleaded.

Dunstan was shaking when he got close, and he looked at me like a parson's wife threatened by a rapist. I was surprised that he was able to speak. He said, "In the name of God, leave us alone. You

115

just killed three Texas Rangers, isn't that enough?"

I was cheerful about it. That sometimes happens to me when the tension is still there and has no place to go. "Not to mention Fallon's two boys. Don't dirty your pants, Mr. Mayor, those weren't Rangers I killed. Those were the Kessler brothers used to ride with Sam Thornton in the old days. Least the oldest one did. Fallon knows all about the Kessler boys."

I pushed Fallon toward the jail with the shotgun. "Speak up, Fallon," I urged him. "While you still got the chance, tell Mayor Dunstan about the Kessler brothers. Do the honors, Malachi—name them."

Fallon gasped out the names—Carl, George, Major.

I told him to explain the Major.

"Major is—was—Tom," Fallon croaked, limping down the street on his busted ankle. "Major's the oldest one. He was a sergeant in the cavalry, but he liked to tell women he was a major when he got out. That's why the Major."

I shoved Fallon into the jail and Dunstan came in after us. I got two sets of irons out of the desk and put them on Fallon, wrists and ankles. Fallon's injured ankle was swelling up fast and I had to squeeze hard to get the shackles in place. "Don't worry about getting gangrene," I told him. "You'll hang just as good with one leg as two. Now, Malachi—you don't mind if I call you that—I want you to tell us those things you mentioned. Don't

116

even think about changing your mind because Dunstan being here won't do you any good. If I decide to kill you I'll do it in the middle of the street with the whole town looking on."

"You got a drink?" Fallon asked.

"One drink—more than that you might get brave," I said. I wouldn't let him hold the bottle. "Now you talk," I said. "You can lie and maybe I won't know about it right away. Later I'll know and then you'll know. Suppose you start with three so-called Rangers riding into town with a murdered boy."

"I swear I knew nothing about the boy," Fallon said. "Sure it was my idea tricking the Kessler boys out as Rangers. Nobody knew the younger Kesslers and Major hadn't been in Texas in years. I wanted to do it the easy way. That's all I wanted, no killing, no big trouble. They'd ride in looking and acting like Rangers, badges and everything, Major doing the talking. You'd step down and they'd take over. Major would figure some way to take Thornton's woman. Maybe say she was wanted on a charge. Even the Eldredges wouldn't go up against the Rangers. How did you figure it?"

"From reading old wanted posters."

Mayor Dunstan looked at me, then at the floor. I think he was losing faith in the big man from Pecos County.

"Look, you're the one to blame," Fallon said. "I didn't come in here shooting off guns and threatening people. Thornton wanted his woman back and that's what I tried to do. A man has the right to

117

get his wife back. I'm telling you I had to do it, but I tried to do it so nobody got hurt. You wouldn't see the sense of that and now . . ."

"And now?"

Fallon got foxy. "You got me set for a hanging charge, Carmody. I ought to get something out of this."

Dunstan looked away while I upended the heavy shotgun. "What you'll get is another busted ankle," I warned Fallon. "Then a busted face. You say what you know and maybe I'll get you run to Mexico when this is over. You were going to tell us about Thornton."

Fallon let loose his surprise. "Thornton's camped two day's north of here with fifty men. It's true, I'm telling you. He was already in Texas when he sent for me. He knew about the Eldredges, how hard it would be to get his woman back. That's why all the men. He figured to make it a slaughter if I didn't think up a better plan. You can't blame me, I tried the best I could."

I told him he ought to get a medal. "How long will it be before Thornton brings his men in?"

"What about Mexico?"

"If what you say is true you'll get to Mexico. Don't ever come back, Fallon."

"That's a promise, Carmody. If Thornton doesn't get word in two days from today he'll be coming in. You want some advice? Everybody get out while there's still a chance. Leave the town or die in it."

I yanked Fallon out of the chair and threw him

back into the cells. "Sit tight, Fallon," I told him, "you're not going to Mexico or any place else. You're going to hang if I have to do it myself."

For the first time since I marched him out of his room, Fallon started to go to pieces. Maybe it was the sound of the key turning in the lock that turned his face gray. "You made a deal," he mumbled, pulling himself onto the iron cot. "You made a deal."

Before I closed the door between the office and the cells, I said, "Never trust a man you don't know. That's the first rule. The second one is—don't trust anybody."

Dunstan was waiting for me to come out; waiting for me and the end of the world. The killings and Fallon's story had scared him so badly, he was drinking my whiskey. I didn't mind about the whiskey—it was all going on Luke's never-paid bill—but I wanted the father of Salter City to stay scared and sober. I took the bottle away from him, had one drink, then corked it with a firm temperance tap. I was good and tired and the big trouble hadn't even started yet.

Dunstan was eyeing the door. "You try to run off and I'll arrest you, Mr. Mayor," I informed the fat man.

A little whiskey goes a long way with nondrinkers. He tried to pull himself together and it wasn't easy with that belly. "I was going to warn the town, Sheriff," he protested.

That was the first time he called me Sheriff without putting a sneer into it.

"It's warned enough," I said. "Go find those storekeepers you brought here the other night. Then you can warn them. Start a panic, Mr. Mayor, and I'll lock you up with Fallon. Conspiracy to abduct a good-looking woman is a serious charge in this state. Siding with a man that got a boy killed could get you hanged. The least you could get is twenty years in Huntsville."

Dunstan had it coming to him, and if I hadn't needed him I would have belted some of the lard off him before I locked him up with his friend. "Do as I say, fat man," I ordered.

He went out of there as fast as his thick legs would carry him. I still felt bad about the dead boy. It was too bad he couldn't have stretched his life a bit longer. It was a shame they couldn't hang Fallon more than once.

I waited for the town fathers to get organized.

CHAPTER TWELVE

They were gathered in my office, but they weren't anything close to organized. That would be my job, and there wasn't much to work with. Leaving out myself, the best man in town—the black- smith—was dead. I sure as hell could have used that blacksmith. Judge Flanders was drunk; maybe he had the best idea in the crowd. Some of the younger men I didn't know looked better than the older men I did know—and that wasn't saying much. I counted twelve men, most of them on the wintry side of fifty.

"Where are the others?" I asked the mayor.

"Run off already, headed south—I couldn't stop them."

"They won't make it," I said. "Fallon says Thornton's moved men around and south of here. Not a lot, a few, enough to stop anybody from getting to the border." That was made up; there could be truth in it. "Even if they do sneak past Thornton's killers, there's nothing south of here but badlands. First Indians, then farther south, bandits. No trails, no water—stop thinking about it, gents. So here we are. The question is—what do we do?"

One of the storekeepers had a bright idea. "You got us into this, you're the sheriff, you think of something."

"That's it," I said. "We'll build a big balloon and fly right over Thornton's head. Don't talk again, mister, unless you got something to say. The rest of you—has the mayor explained it?"

A young fella with no teeth said, "Not so we understand. The mayor says this Thornton is bringing in hired guns to take back his woman. What's that to do with us? Let him take her: she's his wife, ain't she? What do we care what he does to those Goddamned Eldredges? We stay out of his way and he let's us be."

"Thanks," I said. "I guess the rest of you think that's a right smart idea?"

That's what they thought.

"Be all over now if you didn't get in the way," the gummy fella said. "I say, let him take the woman."

122

"What do you think, Dunstan?" I asked the mayor.

"Don't ask me," Dunstan answered.

"Then I'll tell you—you and the others." I must have sounded like a weary schoolteacher going over an old lesson with a lot of backward pupils. "About ten years back, down on the Nueces River, Sam Thornton burned a farmer, his wife and his kids because they made him mad. Thornton's been made a fool of by his wife, so he's madder than he was then. He's so mad, my guess is, that he's ready to kill every man, woman and child in this town. How many people in this town—maybe sixty. Shouldn't take more than fifteen minutes . . ."

"That's crazy," a man said.

"So is Thornton. Besides, he'll have to kill all the Eldredges to get the woman, so why not you? He can make it look like Indians or Comancheros— and who the hell gives a damn about Salter City. Thornton won't want word to get out, that's why he has to kill everything that can talk. Now, friends, you don't like me and I don't like you, but we're here and all we got is two days. You can fight and maybe get killed—some of you will—or you can sit around whining till Thornton's killers get here."

Dunstan looked ready to run again. "That's no choice, Sheriff. We're just a handful and Thornton has fifty hired guns. I haven't shot off a gun since I was a boy."

"You're forgetting the Eldredges," I said.

I had to slam my fist on the desk to shut them

up. "I told you to button up," I warned the gent with no teeth. "Nobody likes nobody else around here. Zack Eldredge hates this town's guts." I grinned at their scared-sheep faces. "So do I. You hate the Eldredges and you're probably right, but, citizens, we—you—need them to stop Thornton. Can't be done without them, maybe not with them."

They started babbling again and this time it was Dunstan who beat on the top of my desk. He spoke to me. "You're new here, you don't know them, they ought to throw in with us—they won't. They won't do it, Sheriff, they just won't. That's their way and nobody can change them. They'd rather fight Thornton alone than side with the town."

"Maybe not," I said, not feeling as confident as I sounded. "I think I can bring them in on this."

I let them talk all they wanted. It was wild, scared, excitable talk; not much of it made sense. For a while, I thought they were going to start work on that balloon.

The mayor tried to suck in his belly; the effort made him red in the face. "You do that, we'll fight."

"Spoken like a man," I said. "Now I want you to round up every gun, old or new or broken, in town. Every stick of dynamite—damn, no dynamite—then every roll of barbed wire. Then I want pine boards and all the six-inch nails you can find. Then shovels and wagon covers and plenty of rope. You got all that, Dunstan?"

The banker had a head for facts and figures.

"Start piling it in front of the jail right away," I said. "I'll need wagons too. Should be back by sundown. I got an important call to make."

If the Eldredges didn't come with the town, it was as good as over. Zack's boys could turn back a first attack with no trouble. In other parts of the state, Thornton couldn't afford to take his time; out here on the edge of the badlands he could sit back and try every sneaky trick he knew.

I rode south at a good clip and turned off to the Eldredge place. Instead of waiting to be shot at, I slowed my horse and started yelling for Zack. I made an awful lot of noise, my voice rolling back to me from the end of the box canyon. I climbed down off my horse and sat in the shade of a big rock, sitting on my heels, my back to the cool stone. They were watching me all right, but they didn't answer my hollers, and they didn't show themselves. It was fine if they thought I was a bit tetched; mountain folk are superstitious about harming soft-headed citizens.

I rolled and lit a cigarette. It was about burned to the end before I heard them coming—tough bare feet scraping over shaly rock. Just like the first time, they came in from all sides; when I looked up from grinding out the cigarette, I was ringed by rifles and wild faces.

"Howdy, boys," I said.

I guess they had no orders to cover a man passing the time of day. They were like hostiles waiting for the only Indian who spoke white lingo to get there. For them that was Zack, and he came loping along on that glue factory nag, the brass framed '66 Winchester shining bright in his hand. He slid off neat and easy for such an old man.

"That's my rock you're squatting under," he started. "My land you're hollering on. I'm getting heartsick of looking at you, Carmody. Now, mister, before I put you in with a lot of hungry hogs will you kindly explain what you're doing?"

He didn't bat an eye when I told him how I'd done for Fallon's two gunmen and the three fake Rangers.

"No big thing with that goose-gun," he stated.

"It's a good gun, nothing like it," I said, thinking of something. "Two big shells, five dead men. You didn't know about it?"

"None of my business, mister. Now if you're through bragging how good you are, suppose you say the rest. You didn't kill Fallon. What'd you do —take his money and turn him loose?"

"Fallon's going to hang for killing a boy," I told him. "Money won't help this time."

Zack's answer to that was a gob of tobacco juice that came close to my boots. "You count on hanging a man like Fallon you're a fool. He'll just buy that judge and jury and laugh in your face. You want him dead, do it yourself."

"That's what I'll do, Zack. If he beats the rope I'll come back and do it myself. Now here's the rest of it."

While I talked, Zack rooted in his pocket for a fresh chew. He had to chase it with his tongue before he could get it under the few teeth he had left.

He was like a sin-hardened reprobate who'd been dragged to church to listen to a sermon. His bitter old eyes were turned in on his own thoughts.

"That's it," I said. "First he'll burn the town and come after you, after your girl. He'll box you in and wait you out. He'll kill you one by one."

"Then let him," the old man said at last. "Maybe he will and maybe he won't. If we have to die, we'll die together on our own land."

I asked him what about the girl.

"I'll save one bullet," Zack said. "Then Thornton can stop looking."

There was an edge in my voice. "Don't suppose she has any say in this?"

"Not a bit," Zack said. "Now, mister, you just been lucky again. What you said about hanging Fallon—or killing him—for that dead boy just saved your life. Twice is the limit. My advice— head south while there's time. You want Fallon hung before you go, fetch him out here and the boys'll do a job on him. Won't you, boys?"

The boys thought that'd be more fun than taking the hide off a Mexican.

"What about money? I don't know how much, that's up to the town. Dunstan and his friends won't argue about price, I'd say. Then there's Fallon's money. You'd be helping save the town, but they'd hate you worse than ever. I guess you'd like that."

The thought of squeezing the banker and his friends had some interest for the old man. He grinned and jetted tobacco spit while he worked it over in his mind.

"They'd never live it down," I prodded him.

"Don't be sneaky, mister," the old man growled. "Playing on my hates won't work. The hell with their dirty money. No more money talk or you'll lose a finger. No more talk about nothing—you just git."

I started to climb onto my horse. "Hold on there," the old man said. "Maybe there is something."

Turning the animal, I said, "Yeah, Zack?"

"That goose-gun," he said. "Five men with two shells, you say?"

"Five men with one shell if they'd been together. A good gun and hard to get. Costs money and not many made. Luke's gun's the second one I came across in a year."

"You say Luke's gun. Then it ain't yours to give away?"

"Sure it is," I said. "Would hate to do it though. You'd like to own that gun?"

"I just might," the old man said. "Got me just about all the other guns there is. Don't suppose you'd consider selling it?"

I grinned and threw his own words back at him. "The hell with your dirty money. Now I got to be going."

That's what I said, but I didn't move out.

"Would have to own it free and clear," Zack haggled. "Put down clear on a piece of paper so Luke can't argue later I stole his gun."

128

I mentioned Judge Flanders. "Signed, sealed, stamped and sworn to, then the gun delivered," I said. "Can't be more legal than that."

"I'll do it," the old man said. "Come on, boys, let's head for town."

Zack was trading their lives for a shotgun; the boys didn't mind. The yelling they started was like Dodge City on a Saturday night in the old days.

Zack waved them quiet with the rifle. "What's bothering you?" he asked.

"I'm the general in this army," I said. "You want that gun, I'm the general. You can be a general too, but I'm the head general. That sound all right?"

Zack had an important question. "What's lard-belly Dunstan?"

I said Dunstan was an assistant private second class. "We'll make him a full private if he works out. Now, General, you round up all the guns and ammunition, then the women, and we'll head for town. You don't want the women out here if Thornton decides to circle around and hit your place first."

I sat on the steps of Zack's falling-down house while he saw the women and the other things loaded into wagons. Sally came out of the house and asked me what in hell was going on. "We're going to argue with your husband," I said. "If it works you won't have to get a divorce. There's still time to kiss and make up so a lot of men don't have to get killed."

It wasn't a serious suggestion; anyway she was

against it. "They'd get killed one way or the other," she said. "Where do you plan to go after this, if there is an after this."

"Mexico," I said. "That was how it started. How about you?"

She looked at me. "I'm thinking about it."

"Next time do your folks a kindness," I said. "Marry a man you can bully. Go north and east— lots of them there."

Zack saw us talking and he came over looking mad. "You, girl, get in the wagon. Ain't no time you ain't shaking it at some man."

"You ready?" I wanted to know.

"Ready enough."

We started off for town, me and the old man at the head of damnedest bunch of scarecrows you ever saw. For some of the Eldredges, boys and men, this would the last time they'd see the old place. They knew that too, but you'd never know from their long silent faces. Ignorant, dirty, pea-brained, vicious, the Eldredges would do fine when the shooting started.

"You got any more unusual weapons you'd like to trade?" Zack was saying.

CHAPTER THIRTEEN

There were seventeen Eldredges and nine men from the town. Old Zack's bearded face twisted into a sneer when I finished the short count. He didn't say anything except with that bitter, town-hating face. Dunstan didn't say anything either; just put out his fat hands and shrugged.

That made it twenty-six men and boys; and there were too many boys and too many old single-shot rifles. Old or new, every rifle carried by an Eldredge was clean as that whistle; the guns gathered up in the town didn't make me too happy. There was some dynamite, none of it new, but it wasn't sweated yet. Dunstan had worked hard to round up the barbed wire and the other stuff—the six-inchers, the lumber, the canvas covers.

I herded them over to the saloon because the jail office was too small to hold all of them. The saloon keeper was one of the runaways, but he hadn't been able to run off with his liquor. Dunstan, the nondrinker, wasn't much of a hand behind the bar, and I went behind the wood to help.

"One drink on the house—that's it," I said for the benefit of the Eldredge boys.

Old Zack knew what I meant. "One drink," he said.

"Later you can drink it all," I announced, free with the coward's liquor—and why not? "Now, gents, here's how we're going to do it. Get in close."

It was a simple plan, but I used a piece of soap to draw it on the mirror behind the bar. I made a sketch of the main street, the only street, the trail coming from the north. The Eldredges were more impressed with my drawing than the rest of the folks.

"They'll come in from the north trail, no reason not to," I said. "Fifty hired gunmen with a crazy man, a killer, at their head. I say that one more time so you won't forget it. They're strong and they know Salter City is nothing, so they won't be too cautious. Now we don't want them to come in too casual because that's too slow. They got to come in fast with Thornton whipping them up. A

132

party of men have got to be doing something north of town, not far, just a ways. This party can't seem like a decoy because Thornton's too smart for that. Let them be doing something, maybe righting a turned-over wagon. They'll see Thornton and they'll run. If they do it right Thornton's men will start after them. Some of those men will get killed . . ."

The men from the town didn't like that; the Eldredges, one and all, didn't give a damn.

"We'll decide who goes later," I said. "The ones not killed will run back to town yelling like bastards. They won't have guns so the only fire will come from Thornton. Then Thornton's men will come charging in to level the town. We let them come in about half the length of the street before we open fire. The first heaviest fire will be from the north end of the street. That way they won't try to turn—they'll ride on through. Only they won't get through because of the two trenches dug in the street."

Zack Eldredge held up his hand. "What is this, Carmody—a fight or a sack race? What's this trench foolishness?"

"Deep, wide ditches dug the width of the street, Zack. Pine boards on the bottom, six-inch nails through them, the top of the trenches covered with wagon covers, with dirt covering the canvas. Where we don't have nails—two-by-fours planed to a point and set in the bottom of both trenches. Pine's not the best lumber for that, it's all we got, it'll have to do."

133

"Then what, Gin'ral?" Zack sneered, and most of his boys hee-hawed about that.

"Some of them'll get over the two trenches," I said. "Has to be. Before they do, coiled-up wire laying hidden to one side of the end on the street will be dragged across the street. By ropes. The ones that go through that won't be much good when they do. The rest of them will turn and try to make it back, and some of them will try to get out through the alleys between the buildings, and they won't get out that way because every opening off the street will be blocked with rocks, barrels, wagons—anything. They won't get out that way, so they'll head back the first way—north. The same thing that end—wire pulled across the street by ropes . . ."

"The damage?" That was Dunstan's question.

I knew they were worried about that; no matter how threatened their lives were, storekeepers never stopped figuring the losses.

"Won't be too bad," I said. "Thornton's men will be mounted on animals that won't spook with gunfire. Got to help them along. We'll start digging and fixing things at first light. Any rider comes into town you tell me you don't know gets locked up, and if he objects to that too hard, he gets killed. Any objections?"

Dunstan looked miserable; I guess he was still a Goddamned banker. "All this killing, Sheriff Carmody—I don't like it. Suppose after it starts they try to give up, surrender, throw down their guns?"

134

"Not likely," I said, "but if the guns get dropped we agree—and then we kill them."

"My God!" the Mayor said.

"Nearer my God to Thee—if we don't kill Thornton," I said. "For Salter City anyhow. No prisoners, Mr. Mayor. We got Fallon. He'll do for everybody. The best way to lose a campaign is trying to guard too many prisoners. Kill Thornton or you'll never sleep safe again. He'll see to that. Now's the time for all good men to turn, unless you want another drink, that is."

Some of the men from the town took the free drink; the rest ducked out of there. Zack, abiding by our agreement, told his boys to take a drink, to find themselves a place to sleep.

I guess the one drink didn't apply to him by his figuring. I didn't think so either. It was well on into the night by then. I was tired and tensed up at the same time; you know how it gets. Everybody was gone but Zack and me—and Dunstan. That fat man was a surprise to me.

The saloon was empty and the night cold came in the door. A night wind stirred the dust in the street and brought some dust in with it. Eldredge and the mayor were in front of the bar; I was barkeeping.

Zack was a silent drinker and so was Dunstan till he got warmed up. "My wife'll kill me," he mumbled.

Zack looked at me, but it wasn't a night for taking sides.

"The funny thing—I'm not afraid," Dunstan burbled.

Zack was using a beer mug to drink his whiskey. I guess when you drink hour-old moonshine a beer mug doesn't seem so big.

"You don't think so?" asked the mayor.

"You ought to be—I am," I said. "Thornton's easy to fear."

That answer got the mayor to laughing; and—when the laughing stopped—hiccuping. "Not Thornton, not him, not him a bit—my wife, I mean. I'm afraid of my wife. I mean, I'm not afraid of my wife."

A painting of some bulging naked lady hung over the bar, above the mirror, and the mayor raised his empty glass, then remembered it was empty, and filled it. He raised it, spilling some of it. "To you, Kathleen, my own," he said, drippy-voiced, quavering, and still spilling fair whiskey.

Dunstan brought down his glass and found his mouth. He got some of it, about half, into his mouth. "You wouldn't understand, men. Around the rugged rocks the ragged rascals . . ."

"Don't take that personal, Zack," I said.

"Not because you say so, Carmody."

Dunstan's glass was full again. "I'll take you home again, Kathleen, me darlin'," he told the bulging lady.

"He must be Irish," Zack Eldredge growled.

Dunstan was staring at the naked lady, the nakedest part there was. For me it was silly as sin, standing behind the bar, the bellied banker and the

136

veralled mountaineer in front of it. I looked up at he bulging lady and winked.

"Certainly not, sir—not Irish but Scotch," Dunstan explained, going at the bottle again. I was supposed to be the barkeep, but I didn't try to stop him.

The mayor turned his bleary-eyed attention to Zack Eldredge. "Do you know the Lady of the Lake, sir?"

"You look Scotch," Zack growled.

"Obviously you do not, sir," Dunstan said, holding hard to the bar. "Sir Walter Scott, sir, that's who that's by. Ruined by the failure of his publisher, he worked night and day, year in, year out, to pay off the debt."

I emptied my glass. "His wife'll kill him."

"Not before I do," Zack Eldredge said. "In a minute, that's what I'll do." The old man's new goose-gun lay on the bar in front of him. Maybe he thought killing the banker was a good idea. Anyway, he put his knobby hand on the gun.

Whiskey made Dunstan a bigger fool than he was naturally. He tried to strut and nearly fell down. "Easy," I said to Zack. "Let the man have some fun. This is Dunstan's night to kick the gong."

"Tell him button up," Zack said.

"Have a care, sir," Dunstan droned. "As a boy I had the honor to serve in the Ohio Volunteers under General McClernand. You, sir, what was your regiment?"

Eldredge showed his few remaining teeth in a snaggled grin. It was a smile that could make a baby go into convulsions. "We stayed neutral in that one, you fat fool. Took on both sides when they climbed the mountain and got in our hair. Took them on and took from them. That was a good war. Sorry it ended so soon."

Before Dunstan could start up again, I told him to go home. The banker hadn't put away more than a pint, but he was ready to enlist all over again. I didn't want to take a grip on his fat neck and toss him into the street. My own drinking had put me in a better mood. I said, "Go home and put that woman in her place. On the double now, Colonel."

The banker liked that. "By Judas Priest, I think I will."

Mayor Dunstan staggered out of the saloon singing about Kathleen.

Zack needed another slopped-over mug of whiskey to wash away the bad taste. It was like water going down a drain. He filled his mug again and asked for a fresh bottle. "Town people—Lord, how I hate them!"

"Think about this," I said. "If there were no towns, then no saloons, no cathouses."

"Make my own whiskey, too old for the other."

"Think we can stop Thornton?"

"Could be hard to do if he comes in the night. You know that, Carmody."

That was what I'd been thinking about sure enough. Big Sam was a town-burner from way back; some men, crazy men, liked the way a town

138

burned bright against a black sky. An oldtime raider with a big price on his head and nothing but a rope from any Texas jury if he got caught, Thornton could be more cautious than I'd figured. Night or day, Zack and his boys would hold and fight till the last bullet; I knew the men from the town would drop their guns and run—they might not even pick them up, but they would run—if Sam Thornton came in the dark.

Old Zack was ahead of me on my next thought, which was to take myself back to the jail and see how Sally was doing. "You want to go, you go, Carmody, nobody's going to get at the liquor with me bedded down in here. Nobody that don't want a bullet in both knees."

I took a bottle and started to leave. Zack's eyes were bright and red-veined and I knew he was drunk. I knew he was drunk because he had to be drunk. "Hold on there, boy," he called after me. "Just one damn minute."

"Yeah, Zack?" Well, I thought, that's what a hungry old wolf looks like when he's trying to be friendly. All along I'd been thinking of him as a dangerous old lobo, but that was just a way of thinking. Most men sort of look like something besides men—bulls, sheep, goats, mules, rats or donkeys. That's just sort of, I mean, but Zack wasn't sort of at all. He was a real wolf.

"You sure you don't want another drink?" Then he sounded that "boy" again. "Just asking because I been thinking."

"About what?" I asked.

"Not exactly thinking but figuring. I was figuring my girl Sally's about to be a widow when this is over. You ain't married, are you, boy?"

"No, Zack," I said. "Guess I'd make a bad husband if I was." I was glad Zack didn't sound too determined. I didn't want to be married by my own shotgun. It was funny, the two of us fairly drunk, there in the cold empty saloon, Sally over at the jail, the mayor maybe kicking his wife in the head, and Thornton out there astride the trail, planning a massacre. I laid it on thick. "Bad isn't the word," I said. "Not bad, meaning I'd be mean to a woman, but, you know—not so young, no money, no settled job. Shiftless, that's me."

"Now don't you downgrade yourself that way, boy. You ain't never met the right woman, is all. Why with a piece of land to call your own, a new house, a few cows, you could raise yourself up in no time."

I looked doleful, ready to drop the bottle and argue with the 8 gauge Davenport if Zack got any more sentimental. "Won't ever be so lucky," I said. "A wandering stranger is all I'll ever be."

Zack dumped more whiskey into his mug. "Don't have to be," he said, more wolfish than ever. "I ain't as poor as I look. Why, son, I could deed you a nice piece of land, set you up with some stock, with all the boys pitching in could raise a house in no time. I ain't Scotch where my little girl is concerned—you could owe me. What do you say?"

"Not now, Zack," I said. "Wouldn't be fair. Less than two days from now we could all be dead."

He wasn't ready to argue about that. It was the best excuse I could think of. And it was true.

CHAPTER FOURTEEN

I had told Sally to stay inside, to keep the door of the jail barred. She was in the doorway sweeping dirt onto the sidewalk, then into the street; and her shape looked good with the light behind her. That started me thinking about Fallon, in the cell next to Luke's homemaking cell. I could take her over to the hotel—there wasn't a roomer in the place—but I didn't want to do that.

She saw me quick enough, and I don't know where she found the broom. It wasn't Luke's broom; Luke didn't think much of brooms.

She swept dirt onto my dirty boots. "Men are

dirty," she said. I stood there, rifle in one hand, bottle in the other. "You are dirty," she said, "dirty and drunk. You're drunk, Carmody. Sometimes I wonder why we women bother."

I was drunk and I told her why. Well, it was the truth, wasn't it? Women always ask why they bother as if they don't know. It's hard on them and it's harder on us. Back East a woman named Woodfin was running for President; and you know where that can lead.

"You got no consideration," Sally yelled, giving a few more vicious sweeps with the broom before she threw it down. "Nothing but dirt, dirt, tobacco spit, whiskey smell, dirt and dunk!"

"I'll take you home again, Kathleen," I said. "What's dunk?"

"You're drunk and Fallon's in there yelling for his supper," Sally said. "Says no lunch nor supper."

"Same for tomorrow," I said. "Be good for Fallon. Too much fat. What're you so mad about?"

"I don't know," she said. "I know and I don't know. You're dirty and you're drunk. I'm in jail and Fallon's in jail. I'm in a worse jail . . ."

I put on my wise face and hiccuped. "Terrible being a woman," I said. "We'll see if we can't stop that."

"Not with Fallon in there we won't," Sally said. "You didn't say Fallon was in the jail when you brought me there. That was a rotten thing, Carmody."

I pushed her aside and unlocked the door to the

144

cells. Fallon got up off his bed, gray-faced by the quick walking and the slamming of the door. For a runner of county politicians and an all-round fixer, Fallon was fresh out of confidence. I guess he thought I had changed my mind and was about to kill him. "Jesus, don't do it!" he yelled scrambling to the back wall of the cell. It was good to see him sweat. I unlocked the cell door and crowded in on him.

"You're bothering the lady," I said before I laid the rifle barrel across his narrow skull. That would keep him quiet most of the night, and if he didn't wake up at all Texas would be a better place to live in. To make him real comfortable, I rolled him under the cot and hung a blanket over him.

I went back outside and told Sally it was time for bed. She came in looking for Fallon. "Shush," I said. "Malachi's finally nodded off."

I wasn't sleepy when we finished what we were doing in Luke's bed. She was asleep when I got back from touring the town, checking the Eldredge boys on guard at both ends of the street. They had nothing to tell me, and the only sounds were the night wind and two coyotes singing a duet. I looked into the saloon and Zack was asleep on top of the bar, hugging that damn shotgun.

I slept in the third cell and Fallon's groaning woke me while it was still dark outside. Fallon dragged himself out and croaked for water. I gave him a mug of cold coffee instead, and told him to stay quiet.

Streaks showed in the sky, and when I went outside Zack was bent over a horse trough, using his hat to pour water over his head. I did the same. The water smelled old, but it was good and cold; what I needed to get my head working. "About time," I said.

We started them digging and rolling the wire before the sun came up. Everybody looked sour or scared, but with sun and coffee to warm them, some of that dropped away. It was the most activity Salter City had seen for years, everybody shoveling and hammering and sawing boards. They got the first ditch dug and floored with spikes, then covered, by nine o'clock. Close up it wouldn't fool anybody but a blind man—or a man riding full tilt through bullets.

They were slower getting the second ditch finished. Dunstan was there digging with the rest, sick as a dog, blowing on his fat hands to cool the blisters. "You're going to have to work faster, boys," I told them. "Still got to block off the alleys and get the wire set up. Set it up, then see if it works."

Zack set his womenfolk to blocking off the alleys while the men worked on the second ditch and the wire. They were finding it hard to get together enough junk to do the job. "Use furniture, anything at all," I said. "Get it good and high."

They had the rolled wire ready to be tested. The wire was rolled around wood frames with ropes going from one side of the street to the other. Zack was saying horses could pull it into position faster than men. I shook my head. "They could spook

146

and pull it too far, maybe clear out of the street. Let's see how fast men can do it."

They tried it. "Not fast enough," I said. "Put another man on it."

They were finishing up the second ditch and everybody looked ready to lie down. It was nearly five in the afternoon and they'd been working for eleven hours with only two short breaks. There were a lot of sour faces when I said it was time to check out their firing positions.

"Soon as we do that it's supper time," I told them. "Every man gets a place and that's where he stays when the time comes."

Zack's boys were the best shots so they got the best places. The ones with the muzzleloaders got the best cover; the men with repeaters would give them cover while they reloaded. Dunstan had a Spencer carbine, a gun I hadn't seen for years. I put him where he wanted to be, at the window of the bank. Zack picked his own spot, the flat roof of the hotel.

I got my horse and mounted up. "I don't want to see one Goddamned face," I yelled in the silent street. Salter City looked like a ghost town, the wind stirring the loose dirt on top of the canvas covers above the two ditches. "I'm going to ride out, then come back in fast," I yelled. "Any man can't get me clear in his sights is in the wrong place. After that—supper."

I rode out and checked the wire at the north end of the street. It was lined up with two wagons end-to-end to hide it. The road from that end of town ran up a slope before it dipped down to level country. Three of Zack's boys were on the far side of the slope with the upturned wagon.

I got to the top of the slope just as the yelling started. Cursing, I yanked the Winchester out of the scabbard. Thornton had jumped the gun and started in a day early. Thornton's column was still riding easy when I topped the hill. It wasn't dark yet, but close—bad light to shoot in. I saw Zack's boys running, Thornton's bunch coming after them, a dark mass of men and horses. I was too far away to give Zack's boys any help.

Thornton's men closed the gap fast. Fallon had said fifty men; there looked to be more than that. Zack's three boys went down about the same time in a hail of lead. One of them got up again and threw a Goddamned rock. A dozen guns sent him rolling. I turned the horse and galloped back toward town. Some fool panicked and shot at me as I came in. I heard Zack Eldredge roaring. I was roaring too. I couldn't leave the horse in the street because he'd spook and run into the covered ditches. Right into the saloon I headed the damn animal, knocking the doors to kindling. Something, maybe the naked lady, made him spook, and with me still in the saddle he started to do a wrecking job on that saloon. He started a player-piano that hadn't played in years and I guess he didn't like the music because he whinnied and stomped the guts out of the mechanical noisemaker before he ran full tilt at the bar.

148

I got the leg he was trying to crush out of the way and rolled onto the bar, then rolled over and off it, the rifle still in my hand. I heard the thunder of fifty or sixty horses coming down the slope into town, then the first shooting. The damn horse started for the front door, then wheeled and charged out the back way.

It was too late to get upstairs where I wanted to be. I ran back to the big window and knocked out all the glass I could reach. I was ready to shoot when the first of Thornton's men rode past with blazing guns in their hands. Hell! There were more than fifty, more than sixty. I shot two fellas off their horses, wounded another fella, but he straightened up, and I had to shoot him again. I shot at another fella and missed and he rounded his horse and started for the saloon door. I was shooting too fast to see the thing hissing in his hand before he threw it—a bottle of Greek fire with a burning fuse. I killed him with one bullet but the bottle landed on the sidewalk.

Bullets chipped wood as I charged out the door and kicked at the bottle. It went off the sidewalk and blew up in a flash of white flame. It showed more of me than I wanted them to see, and bullets came at me thick as hailstones in Montana. Men and horses were screaming in the first ditch, and bullets still came at me, but not so many. Somebody else threw Greek fire and this time it landed inside the saloon. The flames started like a forge with a full draft. Hot as a full-going forge; I could feel the heat from ten feet away. I ran for the hotel, the closest cover on the same side. Horses started after me, then I heard two quick shots, and there was a falter in the gallop. Zack Eldredge stuck his head over the top of the building and yelled at me. I yelled back and kept running.

I made it to the door. A man rode his horse after me, and I guess he wasn't that good a rider, or else the animal was spooked. The horse didn't try to go in the door; he made for the window. The man screamed as he went through the glass, but he was scared, not hurt, when he landed inside in a shower of broken glass. He was quick for a scared man, or because of it. I calmed him down with a bullet in the head. I ran up the stairs, then up other stairs, and out onto the roof.

Zack was thumbing a fresh load into the rifle he had. The goose-gun lay beside him. "Going good, General," he said. "Short notice but good." He ducked his head over the edge to have a look. "There goes the wire."

There was more screaming. I felt bad about the horses. He was right. It was going pretty good; they were coming back, trying to come back. I heard the wire being dragged across the street at the other end of town. I kept looking for Thornton so I could kill him. I knew what he looked like ten years before, but not now, not with the thick light. I might not have seen him at all if Sally hadn't started firing from the window of the jail. That was another thing she wasn't supposed to do. What she was supposed to do was keep the door barred and bolted when I wasn't there, to stay out of the war.

Then I figured what she was shooting at—Sam Thornton.

Thornton was big as they said and he rode straight at the jail on a big Morgan horse, firing as fast as he could pull the trigger. A bullet hit him but hardly budged him. The men, turned by the spiked ditches and the wire, were coming back through heavy fire. Some were off their horses or had their horses shot from under them. Thornton stopped shooting at the jail window and started yelling and pointing. I don't know how many of Thornton's men were left. A lot of bodies were in the street, some quiet, some crawling. Darkness was coming down like a blanket. Thornton threw a rope around one of the beams that held up the jail porch, circled his saddle horn with the free end and backed off the big horse. I aimed and fired and the rifle clicked empty. "Come on," I said to Zack.

I loaded on the run. A wounded man was lurching into the hotel lobby and I used my belt gun to drop him. Zack was ahead of me, the goose-gun cocked to fire. The noise of the porch beam battering against the jail door sounded across the street. Thornton, roaring like a mad bull, was under the front end of the beam, with four men pushing from the back. Suddenly the heavy door burst open and Thornton fell inside. The four men staggered under the beam. They were getting up when Zack, a wild look on his face, stepped up and blew them meat from bones with one blast of the Davenport. Then a bullet took him in the leg and he went down. I swear the old son of a bitch was smiling. There was screaming inside the jail and I went in the door like a bullet. Thornton was crowding Sally into a corner; there was blood on her face and Thornton was hitting her again.

"Thornton!" I yelled. That turned him and I could have killed him, but a bullet would be letting him off too easy. There was a hole in his left shoulder and that arm was no good. He started to jack the rifle one-handed. I put a bullet through his arm, then another bullet an inch lower. He lurched across the room trying to knock me down with his bulk. I got out of his way and tripped him as he charged back. He didn't get far. The butt of the Winchester caught him behind the ear and laid him out.

Outside the goose-gun boomed again. The old man had dragged himself out of the street and was lying with his back to the jail wall, loading and shooting. The roof of the burning saloon fell in with a shower of sparks, but the other buildings hadn't caught fire. The firing had thinned except at the north end of the street where what was left of Thornton's army was trying to break through the wire. Two of Zack's boys came running to pick him up. They kept him on his feet while he loaded a shell into the Davenport. "Now comes the best part," he roared.

They didn't need me to finish the job. It took some doing to get Thornton into the cell beside Fallon. The big man from Pecos County was where I'd put him the night before—under the bed. You never saw a more surprised man than Fallon when he unsqueezed his eyes and saw Thornton.

"You can hold hands when hanging time comes," I told him.

I could hear the Davenport booming up the street, and every time a shell went off the noise drowned out all the other noise. A few scattered shots answered back, then it got quiet. It stayed quiet for a while, and then the big gun sounded again. I grinned at that. Old Zack was making sure nobody got up again.

I went back inside and looked for a drink of whiskey. "That's it," I said to Sally. She took the bottle and drank from it. "You'll be all right," I said. "I said it's finished."

The whiskey made her hard-headed again; three drinks did it. Dunstan came puffing into the jail. "By God, we did it. By God, sir!"

I didn't have to tell him to get out. The fat man was so worked up he could hardly stand still. He ran out talking to himself.

"How long?" Sally asked me. "I mean . . ." She nodded in the direction of the cells. Now there was a devoted wife for you, thinking only of her husband.

"Soon as Luke gets back," I said. "Luke'll get him hanged, Fallon too."

"You won't believe this, but I'm sorry."

"Sure you are."

"You still planning on Mexico?"

"That's right. When I get sick of that I'll do something else."

Spilling whiskey into a handkerchief, Sally dabbed at the blood on her face. "Guess I'll be a rich widow," she said. "Sam has no more rights. I looked it up. I get everything. You want to come to New Orleans, Carmody?"

"I already been there," I said. "Thanks just the same."

"Maybe it's better," she said. "Could hardly work, could it?"

"Not for long," I said. "But we still got plenty of time before Luke gets back. We can sleep late mornings, get drunk every night. I got to wait for Luke and that reward money. Now why don't you take yourself over to the hotel while I check the damage."

"Hurry it up, Carmody," she said when I got to the door.

"I'm back already," I said.

BUCKSKIN

The hard-riding, hard-bitten Adult Western series that's hotter'n a blazing pistol and as tough as the men who tamed the frontier.

#18: REMINGTON RIDGE　　　　by Kit Dalton
____2509-4　　　　　　　　　　$2.95US/$3.95CAN

#17: GUNSMOKE GORGE　　　　by Kit Dalton
____2484-5　　　　　　　　　　$2.50US/$3.25CAN

#16: WINCHESTER VALLEY　　　by Kit Dalton
____2463-2　　　　　　　　　　$2.50US/$3.25CAN

#15: SCATTERGUN　　　　　　by Kit Dalton
____2439-X　　　　　　　　　　$2.50US/$3.25CAN

#10:　BOLT ACTION　　　　　by Roy LeBeau
____2315-6　　　　　　　　　　$2.50US/$2.95CAN

#5: GUNSIGHT GAP　　　　　by Roy LeBeau
____2189-7　　　　　　　　　　$2.75US/$2.95CAN

LEISURE BOOKS
ATTN: Customer Service Dept.
276 5th Avenue, New York, NY 10001

Please send me the book(s) checked above. I have enclosed $ _____
Add $1.25 for shipping and handling for the first book; $ .30 for each book thereafter. No cash, stamps, or C.O.D.s. All orders shipped within 6 weeks. Canadian orders please add $1.00 extra postage.

Name _____

Address _____

City _____ State _____ Zip _____
Canadian orders must be paid in U.S. dollars payable through a New York banking facility.　　☐ Please send a free catalogue.

BUCKSKIN

The hard-riding, hard-bitten Adult Western series that's hotter'n a blazing pistol and as tough as the men who tamed the frontier.

#26: LARAMIE SHOWDOWN by Kit Dalton

____2806-9 $2.95

#25: POWDER CHARGE by Kit Dalton

____2754-2 $2.95

#24: COLT CROSSING by Kit Dalton

____2728-3 $2.95US/$3.95CAN

#23: CALIFORNIA CROSSFIRE by Kit Dalton

____2674-0 $2.95US/$3.95CAN

#22: SILVER CITY CARBINE by Kit Dalton

____2649-X $2.95US/$3.95CAN

#21: PEACEMAKER PASS by Kit Dalton

____2619-8 $2.95US/$3.95CAN

#20: PISTOL GRIP by Kit Dalton

____2551-5 $2.95US/$3.95CAN

#19: SHOTGUN STATION by Kit Dalton

____2529-9 $2.95US/$3.95CAN

LEISURE BOOKS
ATTN: Customer Service Dept.
276 5th Avenue, New York, NY 10001

Please send me the book(s) checked above. I have enclosed $ _____
Add $1.25 for shipping and handling for the first book; $ .30 for each book thereafter. No cash, stamps, or C.O.D.s. All orders shipped within 6 weeks. Canadian orders please add $1.00 extra postage.

Name _____

Address _____

City _____ State _____ Zip _____

Canadian orders must be paid in U.S. dollars payable through a New York banking facility.   ☐ Please send a free catalogue.

PONY SOLDIERS

They were a dirty, undisciplined rabble, but they were the only chance a thousand settlers had to see another sunrise. Killing was their profession and they took pride in their work—they were too fierce to live, too damn mean to die.

_____2620-1   #5: SIOUX SHOWDOWN
                            $2.75 US/$3.75 CAN

_____2598-1   #4: CHEYENNE BLOOD STORM
                            $2.75US/$3.75CAN

_____2565-5   #3: COMANCHE MOON
                            $2.75US/$3.75CAN

_____2518-3   #1:   SLAUGHTER AT BUFFALO
                            CREEK $2.75US/$3.75CAN

LEISURE BOOKS
ATTN: Customer Service Dept.
276 5th Avenue, New York, NY 10001

Please send me the book(s) checked above. I have enclosed $_____
Add $1.25 for shipping and handling for the first book; $ .30 for each book thereafter. No cash, stamps, or C.O.D.s. All orders shipped within 6 weeks. Canadian orders please add $1.00 extra postage.

Name _____

Address _____

City_____State_____Zip_____

Canadian orders must be paid in U.S. dollars payable through a New York banking facility.   ☐ Please send a free catalogue.

Get more bang for your money with special, expanded and double editions of the hottest Adult Western in town...

BUCKSKIN

More action, more adventure, more shady ladies!

BUCKSKIN DOUBLE EDITION: HANGFIRE HILL/CROSSFIRE COUNTRY by Roy LeBeau.

In *Hangfire Hill*, Morgan faces a deadly showdown with a wealthy mine owner's hired guns before he can stake his claim on the Golden Penny Mine. In *Crossfire Country*, he tracks down the killers of a Canadian land baron with the help of a willing Ojibway squaw. Two complete westerns in one volume.

_____2701-1 $3.95

BUCKSKIN SPECIAL EDITION: THE BUCKSKIN BREED by Kit Dalton

This giant volume is the bawdy, blazing story of the Buckskin breed, a passel of children sired by Morgan's father, Buckskin Frank Leslie. Morgan had his back to the wall, put there by a family he had never known. It was brother against brother and the winner would walk away with his life.

_____2587-6 $3.95US/$4.95CAN

LEISURE BOOKS
ATTN: Customer Service Dept.
276 5th Avenue, New York, NY 10001

Please send me the book(s) checked above. I have enclosed $ _____
Add $1.25 for shipping and handling for the first book; $ .30 for each book thereafter. No cash, stamps, or C.O.D.s. All orders shipped within 6 weeks. Canadian orders please add $1.00 extra postage.

Name _____

Address _____

City _____ State _____ Zip _____
Canadian orders must be paid in U.S. dollars payable through a New York banking facility.   ☐ Please send a free catalogue.

SPEND YOUR LEISURE MOMENTS WITH US

Hundreds of exciting titles to choose from—something for everyone's taste in fine books: breathtaking historical romance, chilling horror, spine-tingling suspense, taut medical thrillers, involving mysteries, action-packed men's adventure and wild Westerns.

SEND FOR A FREE CATALOGUE TODAY!

Leisure Books
Attn: Customer Service Department
276 5th Avenue, New York, NY 10001